Sta

ALSO BY COREY J. WHITE

Killing Gravity
Void Black Shadow

STATIC
RUIN

COREY J. WHITE

A TOM DOHERTY ASSOCIATES BOOK

NEW YORK

STATIC RUIN

Cover illustration by Tommy Arnold
Cover design by Christine Foltzer

Edited by Carl Engle-Laird

A Tor.com Book
Published by Tom Doherty Associates
175 Fifth Avenue
New York, NY 10010

www.tor.com

Tor® is a registered trademark of
Macmillan Publishing Group, LLC.

ISBN 978-1-250-19553-1 (ebook)
ISBN 978-1-250-19554-8 (trade paperback)

First Edition: November 2018

For Carlie and Jessica

Static Ruin

CHAPTER ONE

On Joon-ho Station, drifting temple of some ancient religion, the pilgrims press in tight, smell of sweat and grime thick even through my rebreather. The procession moves slow, dry shuffling scrape of footsteps beneath the constant murmur of prayer.

Surrounded by this many people my heart rate should spike, but I'm already soaked with adrenaline after Bianca Blanca sicced her subordinates on me to buy herself time to escape. Now they're strewn along the length of a maintenance tunnel, still breathing . . . barely.

I scan the crowd—hooded black robes, faded to various shades of gray and repaired with patches of darker fabric. Overhead the roof is a huge clear dome. The local star hangs large in the center of an endless field of black, close enough to fill the room with sunlight. Day and night united in a pane of glass.

Ocho is a warm lump in my hood, purring between my shoulder blades. She grumbles when I take her out and stash her in my satchel, but soon settles. I pull the hood up over my head to blend in, and move with the current of bodies. A flash of color and motion catches my eye—people shoved aside, a sharp cry as someone is thrown to the ground.

Got you now, fucko. Blanca knows she's being tailed, but she doesn't know it's by a pissed-off space witch.

I push through the throng, dodging around knots of worshippers, trying to find a balance between gentle and fast. It's been almost a month since I left Aylett Station, fleeing Mookie, guilt, and the Emperor's Guard; the last thing I need is a commotion. The last thing I need is someone recognizing me.

Drop a hollow-moon on a city and suddenly you're public enemy number one. I don't know the price on my head, but even at one credit for every person I killed on Seward, that'd still be a tempting bounty.

I reach a gap, the crowd parting around an older woman sitting on the ground where she fell, another devotee stopping to help her up. The woman seems to hold my gaze as I push past, and my heart goes staccato. They show my face on every news report, and for a second I think she recognizes me even behind the rebreather, but then I notice the white cast to her pupils. She's blind.

She moves off with the other pilgrim, the two speaking Mandarin, and they rejoin the flux circling the shrine, adrift in the smoke of burning incense. I keep moving, offering apologies as I cut through, following the disturbance Blanca makes as she batters her way past the flow of people.

She reaches the far wall and I'm right on her. I grab her collar and yank Blanca toward me. She spins, her face a mask of rage adorned with thin-line geometric tattoos. Glint of a knife blade protruding from between her fingers as she slashes at my belly. I grab her hand with my mind and squeeze. Her eyes go wide at the series of short, wet cracks as I break every bone in her hand. I let go and the knife tumbles to the ground—I kick it aside where it disappears into the forest of feet and robes.

Her mouth shoots open to scream, but the only thing escaping her maw is the sweetly rotten stench of cheap booze. I put a hand over her mouth, push her back, and slam her head against the wall. Her eyes turn hard and she claws my face with her good hand, blunt pain as nails tear my skin. She pulls the rebreather from my face, stops clawing, and stares.

I smash her head against the wall again and grin. "Do I have to break the other one?"

Blanca shakes her head, my hand moving with her face.

"Good."

I peel my hand away slow and she glares at me, rolling her jaw. My satchel shifts as Ocho sticks her head through the opening to stare at Blanca. She yawns and stretches, then disappears back into the bag, circling once before lying down.

"Thanks for the assist, jerkface," I mutter.

Blanca presses her shattered hand to her chest and winces, holding it steady with her other arm. Already the hand is swollen—skin stretched tight over a shapeless mess of fingers.

Her breath turns shallow as she looks at it.

"You'll be fine," I say. "We'll get you to the doc."

Blanca scowls but doesn't resist when I pull her away from the wall.

I fix the rebreather back to my face and we rejoin the procession—easier to float with the current around the huge, sun-lit space than to try and fight against the tide.

. . .

I push Blanca through the door to Doctor Ahlam Ouyahia's clinic, barely able to stay upright, her feet dragging, skin pallid. It's a clean, neat clinic, well lit, every surface white and glossy. We walk through the empty waiting room into the main area, lined with beds along both walls, most of them occupied by patients caught in the dull stasis of illness, overseen by older-model autodocs.

"Ahlam?" I call out.

Her shaved head peers out from the doorway of her office, brow furrowed with concern. "Why is she here? What did you do to her?" Ahlam says rapid-fire as she rushes over.

"She pulled a knife on me, doc, I had to disarm her."

"Why not pull off her whole arm next time."

"I thought about it," I say, and Ahlam scowls.

"You were meant to scare her, not bring her to me broken."

"I didn't know what else to do. Be glad I didn't kill her."

For an instant Ahlam's face twists with anger, then it disappears when she remembers who she's talking to. She lifts her eyebrows and tuts. "Yes, at least you didn't do that."

"She doesn't say much, does she?"

"No."

"Vow of silence?"

Ahlam taps the hollow at the base of Blanca's throat: neat surgical scars. "They say it's one less way to displease the gods. Does not stop her terrorizing me."

Blanca shakes violently, deep in shock—if she knows we're talking about her, she doesn't show it. Doc leads the silent gangster to one of the empty beds along the right wall of her clinic. She lies down with her hand still pressed to her chest. Doc sticks her with a syringe and she relaxes slowly, body melting into the bed, hand falling to her side.

I take a seat near Blanca's bed and Ocho climbs from the satchel to rest in my lap. She starts cleaning herself, body twisted in experimental cat-thing yoga.

Ahlam prods Blanca's mangled hand gently and winces as if they're her broken bones inside the taut red skin. She shakes her head. "I don't know how this will heal."

"Just give her a prosthetic," I say.

"It is not that easy. Besides, she would refuse. Many think those modifications taboo."

"Explains the blind woman I saw."

Ahlam nods absently. She sits beside me and our legs touch. She sighs. We were close once, when she was training to be a doctor, but that was years ago.

"What am I meant to do now, Mars?" she asks.

"Fix her hand," I say. "Tell her if she tries to extort you again, I'll break them both."

"But you will not always be here."

"She doesn't know that."

Ahlam sighs again. "I should not have asked you to do this."

"You needed her off your back and I needed a favor. How's Pale doing?"

"The tests are finished. I was checking over the results

when you came in."

"What's the verdict?"

Ahlam pushes up from her seat. "Come along."

I leave Ocho on the seat and follow Ahlam to the back of the clinic, past her office to the surgery. Pale lies encased within a diagnostic machine, wearing nothing but a paper gown. He's still as pale as his name, but he's grown half a foot since I rescued him from Briggs's flagship. Since I found him trapped inside a hovering weapon platform, wired into the machine to create a psychic blast on command. Fed through a tube, he dreamt in darkness, a skeleton wrapped in skin and nightmares. He looks a lot better now, but he still can't shake the nightmares, and the seizures scare me as much as they scare him.

Ahlam brings a collection of images up on the glass shell of the machine—cross-sections of his skull and brain, spotted with boxes of various sizes, glowing bright in the dull field of his gray matter.

"Honestly, Mariam, I hardly know what I'm looking at," Ahlam says. "I know which part of his brain each of these augmentations is fitted to, but I don't know what they do, and I don't know if they can be safely removed."

"Which is causing the seizures?"

"All of them? None of them? Some combination?"

"Surely that's all in the research I brought you?" The data I stole from MEPHISTO's servers when I was tracking Mookie. Before Seward, before Homan, before Trix died and Mookie was cut open and put back together as part of the hive-mind Legion. Back when it still seemed like I could fix things. Before everything turned to shit.

"Perhaps it is, but I am no specialist. I treat devotees who fasted one day too many, or who prayed until they collapsed. This boy needs a different sort of doctor."

"What can you do?"

Ahlam exhales deeply. "I can give you more medicine to treat his seizures. If you really want to fix him, take him to the people that did this."

Now it's my turn to sigh. MEPHISTO made Pale what he is, and they also made me. They gave hundreds of children telekinetic powers to see if they could make weapons in human form. It worked . . . too well, if I'm anything to judge by. But MEPHISTO is gone. I killed Briggs and every person under his command, and the empire purged most of the witches he'd created.

I want to fix Pale, but with MEPHISTO gone, there's only one person left who can help.

"Your father," Ahlam says, as if reading my mind; "he did this?"

I nod. *Marius Teo.* "Not personally, but it was his research."

"Mariam, you need to go to him."

I groan because I know Ahlam is right, because I've

been avoiding it ever since Sera died. She gave me a picture of him, and I must've looked at it a hundred times since. I don't know how I feel about the man. He made me, but then he sold me to MEPHISTO, knowing they'd make me into *this*, a killer like the galaxy has never seen.

Maybe that's not fair. He didn't make me a murderer; MEPHISTO set me on the path, but *I* killed all those people.

"I can't help the boy, but let me do something for you. You look terrible."

"Thanks," I say, deadpan.

Ahlam shrugs by way of apology.

"I'm just tired. You could give me some metamethamphetamine."

She crosses her arms over her chest. "You need rest."

I laugh, a cold flat noise rising from the back of my throat. I'm about to speak, but I stop myself at the sound of bare feet slapping on polyrubber flooring.

Ahlam's son, Hayreddin, runs into the theatre—all long, gangly limbs and panting breath. He stops in the doorway, sunken chest rising and falling, watching Pale unconscious in the diag machine.

"You should leave him here," the boy says, levelling a cool gaze at me. He has a strong voice at odds with his youth. I don't know where he picked it up from, but he exudes an anachronistic masculinity, acting as though he needs to protect his mother, like she isn't capable of doing that herself.

"What are you saying?" Ahlam asks.

"She needs to go, māmā; they'll be here soon."

Ahlam crosses over to her son and pinches his chin, lifting his head to face her. "Who?"

I don't wait for the answer. I yank open the hatch and the diagnostic machine starts bleeping incessantly. I slip an arm under Pale's neck and lift him, his eyes flickering as he slowly comes to.

"Wake up, buddy, we've got to go," I say softly, pressing his folded clothes against his chest.

"She's dangerous; I had to call them."

"Who?" Ahlam asks again, desperate edge coming through with her words.

"The Emperor's Guard," I say.

Ahlam turns to face me, then looks back at her son. He only nods. I wince when she slaps him, thunderclap of skin on skin.

"You shame us."

"*You* shame us by helping her," he spits back.

Pale finishes dressing, grimace carved into his young face at the argument going on around him. I take him by the hand and start for the door when Ahlam grabs my arm.

"I am sorry."

I shake my head. "He's right. We've got to go." I kiss her on the cheek for old times' sake and lead Pale from the clinic with Ocho following at a trot.

Behind me, the two Ouyahias argue in a mix of Arabic and Xhosa, their voices rising exponentially until I reach the outside hallway and close the door behind me.

I open a comm-link to the ship: "Waren, prep the engines; we've got company."

CHAPTER TWO

Two dozen of the Emperor's Guard line the main concourse leading toward the dock. It's a busy thoroughfare, filled with food kiosks, and vendors selling incense and other offerings for the deities worshipped here.

The Guard move slowly, armed with waver carbines, standard-issue sidearms, and plasma grenades at their waists. The air above them shimmers with the movement of drones. Religious laws forbid perpetual surveillance on Joon-ho—another reason I chose this place—but there's nothing stopping the Guard from bringing their own. They flip over tables and tear down stalls, searching any nook where a person could be hiding. Civilians flee, clutching children to their chests, chased by facial recognition drones. Storekeepers haul their wares away, escaping the imminent wave of imperial havoc.

I pull Pale back into the doorway and press him flat to the wall. He squints like he's calculating an attack, so I squeeze his hand to get his attention. "Leave them to me, alright?" I grab Ocho around the belly, and she swipes at me half-heartedly as I pass her to Pale. "Look after Ocho."

He nods solemnly. "Okay," he says, holding her tight to his chest.

"Stay behind me, and don't watch what I do."

He doesn't answer. I know he thinks he can help, but he's too unstable. If he gets too angry, or too scared, he'll lash out and have another seizure. I can't deal with that now, not with elite troops bearing down and a couple hundred meters of open hallway between us and the ship.

I turn my back to Pale and say, "Hold onto my cloak." He grabs a handful of fabric and I step out of the alcove, walking straight toward the soldiers. Distracted by throwing old people roughly to the ground and separating kids from their parents, the Guard don't notice me until I'm close enough to see myself in the reflective visors of their helmets.

One soldier turns to face me, raising a hand and barking, "Stop!"

I lift him off the ground, feel him as a small dense mote tugging at my mind. He yells when I toss him aside, limbs flailing as he glides through the air and slams into another three troopers.

The rest of the platoon responds instantly, twenty soldiers rounding on me with wavers aimed at my chest, drones gathering above me with camera eyes focusing. My throat spasms in a strangled laugh. It would be so easy to kill every one of them before they moved their fingers off their trigger guards. But then they'd be right about me: Mars Xi, terrorist, mass murderer, heartless creator of mourners and orphans.

I ignore their overlapping orders and start to growl quietly as I gather my thoughts. It's harder to be gentle. First, I crush the drones—the crumpled steel balls sparking as they plummet. Next, I lift the soldiers off the ground, holding each by the throat, squeezing as they squirm and gasp. I drop them one by one as I feel their bodies go limp, weapons clattering to the floor. Hundreds of people along the length of the corridor stare, mouths slack or muttering as they realize who I am.

I never wanted to be famous. Infamous. Whatever.

I pull my hood up and take Pale by the hand. "Hurry now."

Pale beams at the onlookers as we step over the scattered bodies of the Guard. I don't pay them any mind though; I've seen that mix of awe and fear enough times in my life.

We reach the dock and the *Rua*—our Blackcoat-class corvette—sits waiting with its air lock door open. I push Pale toward it.

"Get settled and wait for me." He scratches the back of Ocho's neck and carries her into the ship.

I find the Guard's vessel at the far end of the dock—a Byrne-class destroyer bristling with heavy weapons and stamped with the emperor's two-headed Janos beetle sigil. I grab the ship in both hands and twist. Dull pressure in my head. Piercing screech as the destroyer splits down the middle, reinforced steel plates shredded apart. I drop the two halves to the ground with twin thuds and a clank of debris.

. . .

"I bought us some time," I tell Waren as I drop into the *Rua*'s pilot seat.

"I noticed," the AI says over the quiet hum of ship engines lifting us from the deck.

The cockpit is purely utilitarian compared to the high-tech trappings that Squid installed in the *Nova*. Wide, scratched viewport, stick controls, hundreds of buttons and lights, and the meaty smell of old sweat drifting up from the two seats.

Waren takes us through the station dock, lined with beat-up corvettes and tourist frigates. The engine rumble builds. We punch into the void and my gut drops the instant we leave Joon-ho's artificial gravity.

"Fuck." The word falls from my lips. Three more destroyers wait for us, distant shapes vivid against the backdrop of stars. They're spaced wide, prows tracking us as Waren pushes the throttle and steers away.

"Hold on," Waren says. We turn sharp and my stomach churns again, acceleration twisting gravity as we dive beneath Joon-ho's structure, trying to put the temple-station between us and the pursuing warships.

I swallow a mouthful of hot saliva, resisting the urge to spit or vomit. "Where are Pale and Ocho?"

"They're in Pale's living quarters, already strapped in."

I don't bother replying, I just nod and lean my head back in the seat, fingers digging into the armrest, gripped tight. I key a rear-view onto the main screen and see the cubed structure pointed with shimmering gold minarets growing smaller behind us. The destroyers sink below it like diving birds of prey, sleek hulls shining in starlight.

Lasfire streaks through the void, thud and shudder as the ship rattles, armor plating vaporized, clouds of molten steel visible in the rear-view.

"We need to go *now*, Waren," I say through gritted teeth, watching calculations flash across the nav computer.

Another barrage of laser cuts across the darkness, then blinks out of existence before it can strike—the ships, the space station, the stars disappearing as we fold into worm-space.

"I had the situation well in hand," Waren says with a hint of disdain.

"Sorry," I say. My hands ache and I realize I'm still

holding white-knuckle to the armrest. I let go and flex my fingers. "Where are you taking us?"

"I selected a random point in a distant system. If we make multiple arbitrary trips through worm-space it should make us harder to track. I still won't get to pick our destination, will I?" Waren asks.

I unclasp my harness and lean forward, resting my head in my hands, greasy hair falling through my fingers. I can't remember the last time I bothered to wash it. "Not yet, Waren. But we're doing this for Pale," I say.

"We're going to find your father."

I shake my head. "How did you know?"

"I'm an unnaturally intelligent entity who's read enough of the MEPHISTO documentation to realize that Pale needs specialist treatment."

"Were you listening in on my conversation with Ahlam?" I ask.

"I overheard some of it while checking on Pale," Waren says. "You must have known we were never going to find help at Joon-ho."

"I hoped," I say, but even I can hear my lack of conviction. "Do you have his last known coordinates?"

"Of course," Waren says. "After the series of random jumps, I'll set that as our final destination. Why don't you wish to see him?"

I stand and walk to the cockpit door, pausing in the

opening. "Do you like what you are, Waren? Do you like how you were made?"

There's a long pause, practically an eternity in terms of AI processor cycles. "It's not something I can change, so I haven't dedicated much time to considering it."

"You AI are smarter than any human, but most of us treat you like servants or slaves. Any one of us could unplug your core and do whatever we liked with it. But what if you'd been given an autonomous body?"

"That would be illegal."

"But not impossible. So imagine: what if you had a body? What if people treated you like a human? What if you were *normal*?" Pain festers in that word and a shiver wracks my body.

Waren remains silent, and I can't tell if he's thinking, or waiting for me to finish.

"Teo made me what I am," I say, "but I could have been normal."

"You're better than normal," Waren says, but I can't tell if that's an AI's calculation, or a friend's reassurance.

"There's no such thing as 'better,' there's only 'different,' and people hate what they don't understand," I say, leaving the cockpit behind to wander down the corridor.

And I don't even understand myself.

CHAPTER THREE

I watch the stars beyond the viewport instead of sleeping. We're in a binary system—the two suns locked in a protracted dance, one that will end in flash and fury a billion years after I'm dead.

When I lean back from the port there's a smudge from my oily forehead. I carry my cup of ersatz coffee through to the mess hall, switch the cookstation on, and sit. I start awake when the machine beeps its completion—those unscheduled moments of stolen rest are all I can hope for.

I take the bowl of rehydrated egg-like protein to my quarters and sit on the floor. I spoon food into my mouth—cheesy taste of yeast flakes and salt held together by rubbery bits of I don't even know. The egg-like protein was better on the *Nova*. I'm not sure why; it should be exactly the same.

Before I've finished eating, the twin stars fold away—Waren taking us into another wormhole. I put my bowl and cup to one side and lie on the cold polyrubber, staring at the ceiling.

After Homan Sphere, I can't sleep in beds. In prison I slept on the floor, surrounded by the snoring and farting of the other inmates. Here it's too quiet, the bed is too soft, the guilt is too sharp. The first time I tried the bed after we settled into the *Rua,* the mattress was suffocating. Fear gripped me every time I sank into it, heart pounding and sleep further off than ever.

Now when I try to sleep, I lie on the floor. I did the same thing when I was a kid because I felt like I didn't deserve a bed, I didn't deserve comfort. Don't know how I fooled myself into thinking I did.

At least when I was a child I had nothing to feel guilty for, no reason for the self-loathing that kept me awake.

Even on the floor, I don't really sleep, but I rest. Free from fear with the hard floor at my back, and Ocho curled up on the bed, her slitted eyes watching over me.

. . .

"We have arrived in-system."

Waren's voice comes through loud over the static hiss of falling water. I'm not sure how long I've been dozing in the shower, water filtered and recirculated, kept a steady temperature thanks to reactor heat. I could stay like this forever, pretend that there was nothing beyond the *Rua*'s bathroom, not even empty void.

"How does it look?" I ask, water sputtering from my lips.

"Quiet."

"Good."

I take my time getting out of the shower, drying off, and getting dressed. Walking from my quarters, I put my hair in a loose bun to keep it from soaking the back of my shirt.

When I reach the cockpit, Pale is in the pilot's seat with Ocho curled up in his lap. Her eyes open slightly when I take the other chair, but she doesn't move.

A sphere of green and indigo looms huge in the viewport; Waren ignored minimum safe distance laws to bring us in close. Illegal, sure, but what are they going to do—arrest us?

Gray-black clouds obscure a third of the surface. If there are oceans, I can't see them, or any large bodies of water, just some gleaming white lines that carve through the land—either rivers or mountain peaks.

Sanderak. My father's last-known location. My birthplace. I exhale; chest rattle, heart thud, sick churn in the pit of my stomach, worse than any g-force. I inhale deep and hold it, try to focus on slowing my heart, but it doesn't work.

"What do we know, Waren?"

"Not a great deal; census data is fifteen years out of date."

"Means they haven't let an imperial ombudsman on the surface in all that time. Must value their privacy."

"It could be dangerous," Waren says, "dropping in un-invited."

"Your concern is sweet, but I can handle whatever they throw at me."

"It's not you I'm worried about. What if they damage the ship?" he asks, modulated voice high and innocent. "It's mine once you're done with your errands."

"Asshole," I say, but I'm smiling. *Errands?* If curing Pale's seizures and getting answers to the questions I've carried since childhood are fucking errands then I'd hate to see an ordeal.

"One of the population centers from the census perfectly matches the coordinates for Marius Teo," Waren says, drawing a small square dot on the viewport to mark the location. "I'll bring us down."

A choir of metallic vibrations floods the cockpit, and my ass rattles in the seat as the engine noise climbs. Slowly Sanderak grows larger, filling the viewport and stealing the void from sight.

We hit the atmosphere—constant roar as flames lick at the *Rua,* casting the cockpit in a dull orange glow. The seat turns violent beneath me; I fix my harness then check Pale is wearing his. Ocho leaps out of the boy's lap onto mine, and I curse as she digs her claws into my flesh for purchase. She stands rigid with her back arched, *mraow*ing low and long, barely audible beneath the din. I put a hand on her back to force her to sit, then hold onto her tight.

We keep dropping and the atmospheric burn dies. A billowing black cloud rolls fast across the stratosphere from starboard. It hits hard and the ship lists to port, pitched on the black tidal wave. Sirens blare deafening from the roof, warning lights across the dash flickering in nonsense Morse code. Not a cloud. Black flakes stick to the wide viewport then blow away—ash thick in the air, even this high up.

"Waren, this is bullshit," I say through gritted teeth. He must silence the warning systems because the klaxon stops screeching and the lights flicker and die—cockpit dark, enveloped in the vast plume of ash.

"Sorry," he says.

The *Rua* is deathly quiet with the engines idling, free-falling below the smoke. Once we're clear, Waren blasts us forward. Rich greenery reaches toward the horizon, singed by wildfire. Beneath us, fire fronts scrawl brilliant lines of orange-gold across mountain and plain.

To the north, beyond the smoke, a black lake shimmers in sunlight. We drop again, gently this time. Waren's waypoint grows larger, the square dot now a wide rectangle marking the outskirts of the unnamed city or town. I punch a quick series of commands into the dash, zooming in tight.

There's nothing.

"Waren, can you scan that area?"

There's a pause. "Scans don't reveal anything of interest."

"Damn it," I say softly.

"It might not mean anything," Waren says; "these scanners aren't particularly sophisticated."

"No scanner could miss an entire town."

We come in low, flying just above the treetops. Sunshine cuts beneath the cover of cloud and smoke; the sun slowly setting, painting the sky a gradient of purples and opaque grays. Blue haze drifts from the forest, fields of dry brown grass between tall copses, but still no buildings, no settlement.

Continent-spanning forest fires and smoke-thick air. What if the population fled a dying planet? What if there's no census data because no one lives here anymore?

"Still nothing on scans," Waren says lightly. "Should we try one of the other population centers?"

"No; I want to look around. *Something* was here."

Waren stalls the ship and the nose of the *Rua* lifts, offering a final glimpse of the pastel sky. There's a distant thud when we land and the low whine of the engines shutting down. Huge eucalypt trees with black-dark trunks block the falling sun. Shadows stretch over us, wrapping around the ship—I shiver, blood cold in my veins.

I lift Ocho from my lap, using a finger to unstick her claws from the fabric of my clothes, and give her to Pale. "Stay here and mind her."

Ocho leaps away from him the instant I let go, and Pale stands. He shakes his head grimly and grabs my hand.

"There might not be anything there," I say; "you'll be bored."

"I'm coming," he says in his whisper-soft voice.

"What about you?" I say to Ocho, staring up at me with her eyes wide. "Alright, fine."

I open the locker on the rear wall of the cockpit and grab my rebreather and the child-sized one for Pale. There's a special satchel for Ocho with filtration threaded into the fabric—I put it over my shoulder, but when I try to pick Ocho up she hisses. Someone's getting stir-crazy. I get it though: she's been stuck on ships and space stations for weeks now, maybe months, and no matter how big a station is, sometimes you need to feel some dirt beneath your feet. Paws. Same thing.

"Just try not to die, you jerk." She rubs against my shin and then walks out of the cockpit toward the exit.

Pale and I follow her to the ship's main air lock. I hit

the door controls and the sour smell of sulphur drifts in.

"Fucking 'errands,'" I mutter. I exhale sharply through my nose and shake my head, then fix the rebreather to my face.

Electric laughter fills the ship for a second, but I step outside and the door closes behind me, cutting Waren off mid-ha.

CHAPTER FOUR

I reach the bottom of the ramp and the ship's floodlights flick on with a heavy *chank*, surrounding forest lit stark by the too-white bulbs. Insects flit through shafts of light. Ghost-pale wood is visible where bark has shed, scattered at the roots of the trees like discarded clothes. Birds sing to announce the dusk; trills, squawks, and piercing cries that echo through the stillness.

I walk ahead, dry rasp of grasses brushing against my legs, crisp crunch of dead leaves underfoot. Colossus moths flutter overhead, foot-wide wings glowing with stripes of faint yellow luminescence.

I pull the shard from my pocket, the one containing all the info I've gathered on my father. I check the photo again: his handsome, smiling face, thick forest behind him. They're the same trees, thick black trunks and branches gnarled as ancient fingers. *This is the place.*

"Hey, Waren, could you kill the lights? Gonna have to get used to the dark out here anyway."

Artificial daylight fades to dusk, but the white afterimage persists vivid in the center of my vision. I blink until that fades too.

Ocho rushes through lengths of grass taller than her, either playing or hunting, scratch of desiccated litter scattering at her passage. I make a kiss noise and she trails behind me and Pale as we walk off, still tracking whatever critters she can smell, but staying close. We leave the grassland where Waren landed and move into the trees.

The ground is carpeted with leaves so dry they crumble beneath my step. I adjust my ocular implants for night vision, depth perception dropping until the scene before me looks 2-D, like the forest is an elaborate hoax.

A cold drop of rain hits my arm and goose bumps follow the trail it makes along my skin. I hold my hand out and catch another drop; the water is flecked with black, washing the ash from the sky on its way down. The rain starts to fall heavy, steady hiss building. Pale clutches tight to my waist and Ocho walks a figure-eight around my legs, the two of them treating me like an umbrella. I pick Ocho up and put her into the satchel, then make a shield over our heads. I feel the rain patter in my mind, a phantom shower drumming against my skull from the inside.

Low-slung bushes shake with a strong breeze, and water sprays in under my makeshift canopy. I pull the hood over my head as though it might do something, and keep stalking forward. In my oculars the rain falls like a sheet, my vision filled with static. The rash of movement tricks my eyes and shapes shift inside every bush and beyond every tree.

"Do you see anything?" Waren's voice comes through my comms, dulcet against the sharp noise of the rain.

"Nope. Could have been a city here once, but if one of those fires came through . . ." I shrug even though Waren can't see it.

I pause, resting a hand on black bark, wet and rough to the touch. All I can hear is the rain and my own breath rasping through the rebreather. When I lift it from my face the air is sour—sulphur heavy on the air, with the scent of grass and dry packed dirt yielding to the storm.

The rain stops just as suddenly as it started, the torrential downpour reduced to a light spattering then gone altogether. The clouds overhead disperse and moonlight shines through.

A new shape rises from the darkness: a glass dome glowing dully from within. Stalking quiet through the forest only to find a mysterious glowing dome feels like a trap. *You want to trap me? You don't know who you're messing with.*

Ocho sticks her head out of the satchel, her eyes wide black saucers. Pale points to the dome as though I could have missed it, visible in shafts between the trees.

"Come on," I whisper.

He reaches out to take my hand, but I shake my head. He's been around me enough to know what that means: I need to be ready for anything.

I creep toward the dome, every step carefully placed, waiting for the trap to spring. We leave the tree line and the structure stands before us in the middle of a circular meadow. I disable my night vision: a dim shape lurks inside the structure, its edges contorted by the bend of glass.

We dash across the hollow field. There's a hatch built into the dome, a panel between two metal struts with a thick steel handle. I pull it open with a piercing shriek of rusted hinges, and step inside with Pale close behind.

The floor has been dug away, polycrete laid three meters beneath ground-level, with wooden stairs following the side of the dome and leading to the landing below. A statue towers over us, lit from all sides. It's a figure cast in sallow white: a woman with cascading hair, sculpted fabric flowing from her as if caught by the wind, and one arm resting on a swollen belly.

"It's you," Pale says, breathless.

I glance down at his furrowed face, and look back. I'm about to argue, but then I imagine I'm him, looking at me from below.

He's right.

She has my jaw, my nose. She has the overly long neck I was self-conscious about for most of my teen years.

My chest tightens, blood strangling my veins. My breath goes fast and shallow, head light as tiny black spots encroach on the edges of my vision. Mediag suite flashes a warning on my ocular Head-Up Display, but I don't read it, I just keep staring.

It's not stone like I'd first thought, it's wood—the pale flesh beneath the black bark of the eucalypts outside. The woman's legs—*my legs?*—grow from the dirt, two living trees, somehow twisted and sculpted into this effigy.

Pale grabs my hand and tugs at it. I pull my eyes away from the statue's face slowly, my other senses returning as a distant part of my mind screams for attention. I hear the noises then, the clunks and clanks of armed people approaching—a sound I know too well, a sound that woke me every morning as a child, and many mornings since.

They stream out of the tunnels like ants; fifteen or so women, a few men, and some others. Most have guns—ballistics, lasers, and wavers—the random assortment of a militia, rather than an army.

I raise my hands slowly and hold them up, mind tingling with readiness, the statue in my likeness forgotten for the moment.

The leader removes her rebreather, revealing a thick-featured face, olive skin, and deep-set eyes. "Get down here," she says, voice resounding from the dome walls. "Slowly."

I chuckle quietly and the noise vibrates in my rebreather. I lower a hand glacier-slow to take hold of Pale. "It'll be alright."

"I know," he says brightly. He lifts his free hand to his mouth to whisper conspiratorially: "Should we kill them?"

I crouch and hold his gaze. "No, Pale. Never unless we *need* to, alright?" Apparently I've been skipping the ethics part of our telekinetic lessons.

"I said 'slowly,' not 'ignore me,'" the woman calls out.

Pale and I walk down the polished wooden steps, tracked by suspicious eyes and all those weapons. We stop when we reach the bottom; behind the gathered crowd, dimly lit tunnels curve off into darkness.

"Who sent you?" the leader demands. She doesn't wait for an answer before barking, "Check them for weapons."

Three women peel away from the group and step forward. Two are armed and they stay back, one gun aimed at me, the other aimed at Pale, while the third approaches to frisk us. She's pure genefreak, a mass of muscles rippling beneath heavy overalls, gills neatly lining both sides of her neck.

"Be gentle with him," I say, noticing the rapid rise and fall of Pale's chest.

The woman checks under Pale's arms and down his sides, her massive paws large enough to wrap around his whole torso. Pale scrunches his eyes closed and breathes loudly, trying to push the woman from his mind—a technique I taught him to help him disassociate.

"What's in here?" the genefreak asks, reaching for Ocho's satchel. I was so worried about Pale, I forgot about that little terror.

"I'd leave it if I were you."

The woman looks at me with open disdain and reaches for the clasps.

The instant the bag opens, Ocho flashes out with a *rawr*. Claws extended, she latches onto the woman's arm, biting and scratching viciously. The genefreak screams and stumbles back, her two guards bringing their guns up.

"No!" Pale yells. Ocho leaps free just as Pale's psychic blast tosses the women aside. Ocho lands on all fours with her hackles up, the tiny beast puffed out fiercely.

There's a clatter of guns being cocked, loaded, and charged as the rest of the militia reacts. I inhale deep and throw my arms out; each person a grain of sand, lifted up and tossed aside. Some crash into the statue, others strike the dome hard, impacts leaving cracks in the glass.

I grab Pale by the shoulder and spin him toward me, press his face into my stomach. "It's alright," I say, then I pull the rebreather from my face because it's hard to be comforting through a mask. "It's alright. No one's going to hurt us."

There's a loose chorus of groans as people push themselves up from the ground.

"Just leave the guns where they are," I say, "and no one has to get hurt. I am a tired, irritated fucking space witch, and right now I've got some questions that need answers. Like, why the fuck do you have a giant statue of me in here?"

Used to be a time when I hated labels like "space witch," but honestly, it's better than "mass murderer."

The leader brushes at her clothes and walks over, stopping close. Her eyes are soft now, but intense, darting within their sockets as she studies my face. Behind her the others peer at me with jaws slack, glancing to the statue for proof or guidance. One of the men starts crying, hands clasped and pressed against his lips; others whisper quiet prayers.

Ever since Seward—since the authorities condemned my actions and the media plastered my face on every screen across the galaxy—I've gotten strange looks. The few people who have recognized me have fallen silent, turned pale, run, or some combination thereof. But this? This is different.

"Stand down," the leader says firmly; "she's one of us."

CHAPTER FIVE

"I don't believe it." The woman extends a hand to touch my face, but stops short and lets it drop to her side. "Sorry, how rude; I'm Dima," she says.

"Mars."

"Oh, we know who you are now. With the mask . . . we couldn't tell. You'll want to see him right away."

I swallow hard and a blunt ache travels down my throat. *I'm not ready.* "Sure," I say, the single word strangled from my vocal cords.

Dima turns and dismisses the group. They linger and continue to stare, then collect their weapons and slowly pull away one at a time. They wander down the corridors beneath the dome and disappear into the shadows.

"What did you mean when you said I'm one of you?" I ask Dima. She's older than I am, by ten years at least—older than any of the girls in MEPHISTO's facility when I was a child.

"Marius began his experiments here. Many of us are Teo's Sons and Daughters." My shock must be obvious, because Dima shakes her head. "Not like that . . . there were only the two of *you*. It's simply what we call ourselves."

"Teo's heirs," I say under my breath.

"And what a grand inheritance he gave us," Dima says.

I nearly laugh, but stop myself when I see her severe sincerity.

"Come; let's go." Dima rounds the statue, brushing the wood with her fingertips. She stops and waits in the mouth of a tunnel.

I rub my hand over Pale's head, short blond hairs pushing back against my skin. "You feel okay?"

His brow furrows and his eyes scrunch in thought. He shrugs.

"If you feel like you're going to pass out, let me know. Where's Ocho?"

Pale points to Ocho digging in the loose dirt at the base of the statue, covering her shit so it won't give her away to predator or prey.

"You couldn't have done that outside?"

She glances up at me, paws still busily working in the dirt. When Ocho's done I put her and her filthy paws back into the satchel before she can desecrate anything else.

We join Dima in the tunnel, now lit warm yellow from tiny bulbs embedded in the polycrete walls. Dima walks slowly, hands clasped behind her back, her eyes black pits in the dim light.

"The boy is . . . like us," Dima says. When she's not barking orders her voice is caramel smooth, flow unsteady, overlong gaps between some words.

"Pale. I mean, that's his name. I brought him here to try and get help. He has seizures when he pushes himself too hard."

Dima hums. "We don't have that problem with our boys. I don't know . . . that we'll be able to help."

"But Teo might."

"Marius might," she agrees.

It's strange to hear his name spoken with such awe. To me it's just another name. I never had a "mom" or "dad," no one to wear those hallowed titles.

The tunnel winds and splits, branching in various directions, each intersection marked with signs like you'd find in any city.

"You built a whole city underground?"

"Not exactly," Dima says. "We buried it."

She pauses in a cavernous space. Here, polycrete gives way to soil, walls lined with tree roots like knotted lengths of hair. The chamber is roofed in hardened x-glass—drifts of ash roll across the curved surface and starlight shines through, silhouettes of trees swaying in a breeze we can't feel here under the earth.

"The wildfires," I say.

She nods. "We couldn't fight them . . . and we couldn't afford to rebuild every time one came through. Simpler to reinforce where needed, build tunnels, and bury the rest."

"Smart," I say.

"It was his idea, of course."

"Is there a dock someplace I can store my ship?"

"There's a hangar beside the Governor's Residence. But surely it can wait 'til morning . . . it's a long walk back."

"I've got a chauffeur," I say with a smirk.

"In that case."

Dima bursts me the dock coordinates and I pass them on to Waren with a note telling him to be careful. Statue or no, Marius or no, I don't trust these people.

• • •

The tunnel slants downward, taking us deeper underground until we reach a set of wide stairs. At their base we come to a huge courtyard outside the Governor's Residence.

A building as large and important as this would normally use height to impose on the landscape, but in the buried city of Sommer they had to take a different approach. The mansion's dark façade is hewn from stone and veined with constellations glittering in shades of silver, blue, gold, and brass. Set deep into the cavern, it looks like an ancient tomb uncovered by archeologists rather than a building recently interred. Pyrite columns support the roof of the world, shimmering orange-red-yellow with reflected fire from burning pillars around the courtyard. The sharp smell of kerosene lingers despite the constant hum of air filters, audible over the flickering of the flames.

The doors to the mansion are huge slabs of white timber, polished to a molten sheen and etched with intricate geometric patterns, bordered with words in a language I don't recognize.

"He's expecting us," Dima says. She extends a hand, offering for me to go first.

I nod her forward instead. "I insist," I say, smile stretched across my face like a death mask.

"Very well."

Dima walks ahead, seeming to grow as we approach the door—her back somehow straighter, chin raised.

I follow her inside, holding Pale's hand firmly when he clutches at mine. We could be inside a lavish house on any world in the imperium: large and well lit, decorated in a way that speaks to wealth but not necessarily taste. Walls adorned with abstract art, boring as it is inoffensive.

Behind me, Dima says, "He has asked for a few more minutes. While we wait, perhaps you would like to see her."

"Her?"

"Your mother."

My heart sinks and swells, rattles my rib cage with jackhammer pounding. "I—I don't—"

"She's through here."

Dima walks deeper into the house and I wait in the foyer—not so much hesitating as stuck in place. Pale pulls at my hand and I let the momentum move me. We trail Dima down a long corridor, walls glinting with gold damask. She opens a heavy translucent door and a heady floral fragrance wafts from within.

The room is a cube of white, containing a smaller glass cube in the center of the space. Terran flowers surround it on all sides—lilacs, tulips, frangipanis—every petal white. I drop Pale's hand and walk in slowly, legs struggling to carry me closer to her.

It all makes sense now, the statue, the looks of awe. My mother sits preserved behind the glass, dead. Except she's not my mother, she's me. I could be looking into a dirty mirror. Her hair is black, with gray streaking from her temples, collected in a bun like the one I'm still wearing. Fine wrinkles scatter from her eyes and mouth, only visible when I stand right at the glass, pressing my palm against the cool surface, my breath gathering as condensation.

She's sitting in an ornate wooden chair with hands clasped in her lap. There's no tattoo on the back of her right hand, no brand to delineate her within an experimental program, but otherwise we look . . . *exactly* . . . the same.

I'm a clone.

CHAPTER SIX

I drop to the floor and sit cross-legged, flattening a stand of tulips, eyes still stuck on my mother.

Ocho climbs out of the satchel and into my lap. I don't even stop her kneading my flesh with her claws, too struck by what's before me. When Ocho stops and settles, I rest a hand on her back and absently stroke her long gray fur. "I guess we're both clones of our mother."

"You didn't know?" Dima asks from the doorway.

I shake my head.

"You were always more than just a clone," Dima says. "You . . . were the culmination of all Marius's work."

Pale knocks on the glass, as if testing that the woman is really dead. He looks from her to me, not scared or confused, but curious. "Mars?" he says softly. "Is there another one of me somewhere?"

"I don't think so, little man."

He considers this for a moment with his lips pursed.

"What was her name?" I ask Dima.

"Cilla Jiang."

I sigh. "She's not really my mother."

"She carried you; she died giving birth to you. She was . . . as much a mother as any could be."

No one should die in childbirth, not today, not with access to even the most rudimentary medical facilities. I lean my forehead against the glass and let my eyes land on Ocho, pushing her head into my hand so I can scratch her chin.

"If I'm her clone then my father's not my father."

"You were a daughter to him; he loved you, you and Sera both."

"Don't you dare say her name," I spit, my face twisted in rage and anguish, vision blurred by tears.

"Forgive me," Dima says. "I remember her. I was maybe nine when she left, and she was a toddler . . . but I remember her. Not you though. I don't know why."

"Because Teo discarded me the moment I was born. But sure, he loved us so fucking much."

I smack the glass with the base of my fist. I'm not trying to break it—for that I'd use my mind—but I need to hit something, and the slow thudding beat gives structure to the maelstrom of thoughts roiling through my head.

What little I knew about my past is a lie.

"What was she like?" I ask. "Sera?"

"She was kept away from the rest of us because she was special, but she'd break out of your father's lab when she wanted someone to play with."

I give a wry smile. "Breaking out was one thing she was good at. What about my mother?"

Dima hesitates. "It's not my place to say."

Sealed under glass like a fucking butterfly on display. Whatever she was like, I'm sure she deserved better than that.

"Do you have any video, audio; anything that might help me get to know her?"

"Of course," Dima says. "I'll see what I can gather."

"I was hoping to find you here."

I spin at the man's voice—low-pitched, oozing smug condescension. It suits his face perfectly: hooded eyes, small nose, thin lips pulled back in a certain smile—a face you want to punch. He wears a white robe hemmed in mud and stitched in gold thread. I grab Ocho and put her on my shoulder. She climbs into the hood of my cloak as I push up from the flower bed.

"Who are you meant to be?" I ask, brushing dirt from my ass.

He presses his hands together and bows; I barely stop my eyes from rolling.

"Neer Dehner, acting planetary governor and assistant to your father. I took on the affairs of Sanderak so that he could focus on his work." He places an odd significance on "he" and "his," as though the words were naming some god.

"How noble of you," I say deadpan. He reacts as though I were sincere, nodding his head to one side.

"The people here view him as a father figure and more. He would get little done without an intermediary."

Intermediary or high priest? I think, eyes scanning his lavish robes once more.

"Before I take you to see your father, shall the four of us share a meal? We have a variety of unique fowl here on Sanderak, and my personal chef has recipes grand enough for the emperor themself."

Pale looks at me expectantly. I'm as hungry as you are, buddy, and I've had nothing but prison slop and travel food for months, but... "We'll take a rain check; I've travelled too far and been through too much shit to wait any longer."

He bows again, his eyes distant when he straightens. Moments later, four guards appear in the hallway, carrying ballistic pistols and wearing body armor beneath cloaks fashioned like Dehner's robes—white with gold filigree suggesting the soft curves of a moth's wing.

"Would you like me to take her?" Dima asks.

"No, thank you, Dima; I'll take Mars to see him."

"She should know the truth."

He quiets her with a glance. If I didn't dislike this guy already, the harshness of that look would have done it.

"The truth will be made apparent in time. Come, he is ready for us now."

I turn back to Cilla Jiang, take in my dead and future self once more, then leave the floral mausoleum with Pale by my side and Ocho weighing heavy in my hood.

Dima closes the door after us; it seals with a beep and the clank of a locking mechanism. She stays behind as Pale and I follow Neer and his guard to the rear of the Residence. We exit through a door leading outside—if an underground cavern can be called "outside."

"Marius spends very little time within the Residence," Dehner says. "He has an affinity for nature and the natural. He says he feels connected to the heart of Sanderak when he has his hands in the dirt."

It's dark here, darker than the front courtyard, lit only by fireflies massed on the high curved walls. Tree roots fall from the ceiling to form thick columns, lining a path further into darkness. Underfoot, polycrete gives way to packed dirt, and Neer stops, flanked by his soldiers.

"His sanctuary is just ahead. I'll wait here with the boy." Dehner holds a hand out toward Pale, but he puts an arm around my waist and squeezes.

"No," I say, "he'll stay with me."

"Very well. I'll warn you now," Dehner continued: "he won't be what you expect."

I can't tell if it's a threat or a warning, but I ignore it either way.

Ahead, two trees grow from the ground, ghost-eucalypts that twist around each other to form an arch. At the apex they break apart and spread like antlers reaching toward the earth overhead. Pale and I pass beneath and into Teo's chamber.

Within the sanctum the roof is open to the night sky, near-full moon edging across indigo. Flakes of ash drift through the gap, carried untold distances from the perennial fires that burn across the planet. Tree roots run thick through the walls, holding the earth in place as well as any man-made material would. There's a rich smell of earth, the green scent of dirt and moss, the smell of a damp grave without the rot of a body.

A man stands in the middle of the weakly lit space, hair in loose gray curls, long enough to rest on his shoulders. He stares at his open palm where a colossus moth rests, wings outspread, dim glow lighting his face from beneath.

"Welcome, my children," he says, without looking up. It's a smooth voice, calm.

"Do you even know who I am?"

"Of course I do, daughter." His eyes glint when they fall on mine, and he smiles warmly.

"Mars," Pale says, clutching tight to my arm, "I don't

like it here." His eyes trace over the cavern, pupils shimmering with the reflected light of fireflies.

"I won't let anything happen," I say softly. I pull my arm from Pale's grip and step forward, holding a hand out so Pale knows to stay back.

Teo watches me absently, his face calm.

"Tell me why I shouldn't kill you."

"We are not about death here," he says, "we are about life. We come here to celebrate life, to . . . create it."

"Sure, create life then toss it aside. Sell it to the highest bidder. Let them turn children into fucking monsters."

The same smile again. "None of my children could be a monster."

I try to laugh, but it comes out like a cry. "Tell that to the people I killed, to their families," I say, guttural thick, oddly painful after the high shriek of my laugh.

I leave Pale behind and step closer, close enough to see the individual strands of his hair and the pattern drawn in the furry wings of the massive insect still resting on his hand, unperturbed by my approach.

"Family is truly important. I was gifted with unconventional children, ones that I had a very deliberate hand in creating, rather than relying on the lottery of conception."

"What are you talking about?" I ask with barely contained rage, as all the years of hurt and anguish bubble in my mind; gray matter humming, thoughts turning to violence.

I cry again as anger sears through my mind. My thoughts strike out and dirt shakes loose from the wall behind him, but Teo doesn't flinch.

"What is—" I step forward and throw my arms out to shove him—physically—and stumble through empty air. Bright colors flare across my eyes, then I'm through him, through the hologram. Balance regained, I spin and Teo is there, smiling kindly, moth still resting in his hand.

I walk through the hologram, throwing an arm out as if to push it aside but instead slamming the wall of Teo's chapel with my mind, crashing a ton of dirt into the hallowed space. I hold out my hand and Pale grabs it, marching quick beside me as I storm out beneath the archway.

Dehner's honor guard has already formed up in front of their charge. I point a finger at Neer and yell, "Tell me why I shouldn't kill you."

The guards raise their weapons and open fire.

Their faces light up in split-second muzzle flash, hand-cannons booming loud in the confined space. I could have stopped them, could have tossed them aside before they fired—instead I flick my wrist and push the bullets aside, dense slugs peeling away to thud into the wall. A growl builds in the back of my throat, but in that moment Pale doesn't hear it, he doesn't know I'm ready to deal with the guards. He lashes out. The ground explodes beneath them, dirt, rocks, and people thrown high. One of the guards slams into the ceiling—something inside him snaps and he cries out in pain before he hits the dirt.

Pale's eyes roll back in his head, irises hidden. He crumples.

I lift Neer from the ground, hand outstretched and twisted into a claw as I choke the life from the slimy shit-stain disguised as a man.

"Tell me why I shouldn't kill you," I repeat, screaming. Through the film of tears Neer is little more than a white blur on black.

"I can explain everything. I can tell you where he is," Neer begs, choking the words out in a broken, slowing rhythm. His words mean nothing, less than nothing, but I let him go. He collapses to the ground, a sodden pile of robes and man gathered on the ground. I drop to my knees to hold gently onto Pale, seizing in the dirt.

"Hey, hey, it's me, I'm here, hey." I keep crying, but it's different now. The rage is gone, replaced by fear and something like love for the boy who's shaking and hurt. "Pale, please, hey, it's Mars. I'm here, okay?"

CHAPTER SEVEN

The Governor's Residence is quiet. If Neer and his security officers followed me back inside, I didn't notice them, my focus wholly on Pale.

He lies on the mohair lounge, his head resting in my lap, eyes staring blankly at the ceiling. Ocho is a perfect circle on Pale's belly, purring softly in her sleep.

Dima approaches quietly with a small stack of clothing pressed to her chest, which she sets down on the couch beside me. "I found some clothes that should fit him—I noticed his were getting a little small."

"How are you doing?" she asks Pale.

He smiles but doesn't speak.

"Do you need anything? Water, food?"

He nods, excited, but when Dima looks at me I only frown.

"What happens next?" I ask.

"What do you mean?"

"You *know* what I mean." The man that Pale hurt, my attempt—and remaining desire—to harm Dehner. Things might have stalled with Pale's seizure, but I'm still waiting for the storm to hit.

"We'll go for a walk and . . . talk it through."

She sounds calm, but I burst a message to Waren just in case; if we need to make a quick getaway, I want him ready.

· · ·

It's past dawn before we leave the residence, and sunlight falls in shafts through holes in the roof of earth over Sommer. A local could probably read the time from the angle of the sun, but I have no idea. My eyes ache with fatigue, black bags beneath them like I've taken a beating.

It's bright for a subterranean city, green-blue sky visible through the wide holes. These openings are lined with steel-retracted covers ready to extend over the gaps in case of a passing fire.

Pale carries Ocho in his arms as we follow Dima down broad corridors. Townspeople whisper and stare, some openly, some subtly. At least here there's a chance they're talking about me in relation to Cilla or Marius, instead of all the dead on Seward: over three hundred thousand, according to imperial media.

We stop in a wide town square, steel roof retracted, leaving the plaza open to the firmament. Each wall is dotted with tunnels, and I guess it's a central node for Sommer. A fountain dominates the center of the space, a shallow pool with a statue of Marius standing in the center, the stone man surrounded by adoring stone children.

In the far corner of the square, real children are gathered, overseen by three women around Dima's age.

"Where are we going?" I ask Dima.

"That depends . . . on you." She points to one tunnel. "I can take you to your ship right now and you can leave. Otherwise, if you promise to remain calm, I can take you to lunch with Neer. There is much for the two of you to discuss . . . if you can do so with civility." She emphasizes this final word, letting it float through the gap between us and find its faults with me, with my violence and anger.

"I'm not leaving without answers, without help for Pale."

"I understand that, but you must realize how frightened Neer is."

I'll give him something to be scared of.

"I won't apologize. I don't appreciate being toyed with."

Dima sighs. "Come over here, I want to show you something." She walks toward the class of children. Pale follows her immediately, then stops to look back at me. *Alright, fine.*

Dima stands with her hands behind her back, admiring the students' work. Boys and girls sit cross-legged in the shade of the reinforced earthen wall towering above them. Each one is painting a tree—black trunk and twisting branches, some with leaves in variegated green, others burning with watercolor flames. Every hand is empty, brushes clasped by their minds.

"That's incredible," I say, and it comes out cynical and ironic, but I mean it. I can kill an army with my thoughts, but I'm not sure I could do this: the finesse needed for such fine line work, the gentle touch it would take to use the brushes without breaking them.

I see Dima in the corner of my eye, watching me intently. She turns back to the children. "Neer was foolish to think Marius's . . . avatar could deceive his own daughter. He shouldn't have lied, but this is why he does it. Sommer is a safe place for people like us, for the children, and Neer will do whatever he can to keep it that way. We have to hide here, for our own safety, but if the people of Sommer know Marius is gone, they will search for him.

"Out there . . . people only want us as weapons, but we can be more than that. We can teach the children to do more with their powers than kill."

It feels like an accusation, but when I look to Dima she's smiling sweetly at one of the girls in the front row. Just my guilt manifesting.

"Is that your daughter?" I ask.

Dima nods. "We pass our gifts on. Some of our chil-

dren are stronger, some weaker. Marius said that
MEPHISTO . . . augmented you to boost your power.
Without those augmentations our abilities aren't suited
to your scale of violence, but we . . . still need to teach the
children to respect the power, and each other."

"Who else knows about you?" I ask. After I escaped
their facility, MEPHISTO tracked me for seventeen
standard years. And here's a whole town of telekinet-
ics, ready to be harvested for some new research program. Nausea churns my guts at the thought.

"No one," Dima says.

"You think some cute kids will make me forget all the
other shit? My dead mother in a creepy glass box, that
hologram parading as my father? Where is he, really?"

"That is what Neer would like to talk to you about."

"Fine," I say with a sigh. "I'll meet with him."

"Thank you, Mars. When you speak with Neer . . . remember that we need you. He might be too proud to admit it, but I'm not. Let's go now."

She takes a step away, but I stay put. "How do they
hold the brushes like that?"

Dima chuckles. "Didn't you pull a moon down from
orbit?"

"It was hollow, so it barely counts."

"How did you reach something so far away?"

"I imagined it was close enough to grab."

"Right," Dima says. "It's a matter of perspective. If you imagine you're holding something small and . . . awkward, that's exactly what it will be."

Dima looks over the gathered children once more, her eyes pausing when they fall on her daughter. "You made things so much harder for them."

"I know," I say. Add one more hurt to the fucking list.

CHAPTER EIGHT

"I apologize for lying to you, Mariam," Dehner says, face blank, no hint of remorse in his voice.

I don't bother to stifle a long yawn; it seems like the only response he deserves.

"I was curious to see how the avatar system would re-act to someone who knew—who had history with your father. Obviously it was a mistake."

"You'd have been screwed if we were a hugging family," I say flatly, and Dehner laughs.

We're sitting opposite each other at a large dining table, ghost-wood surface polished like a dull mirror. Dima is beside Dehner, and Pale sits opposite, devouring every plate of food that's put in front of him—fuel for his next growth spurt. I don't know how he compares to other boys his age, if being strapped into that weapon stunted his growth, but he looks happy. That's got to count for something.

He takes a shred of slow-cooked meat from his plate and feeds it to Ocho, sitting on his lap but hidden under the tablecloth. A smile briefly crosses my lips and for a moment I forget about Dehner and his muted reflection talking at me.

"It's a simple system, really," Dehner continues, raising his voice to recapture my wandering attention. "A database containing everything he ever wrote, and every visual and audio recording we could find. It uses this information to generate new insights, answering any question as though it *were* Marius. It's as accurate a distillation of his public persona as it is possible to create. I know it's a deception, but the avatar gives people hope."

No one is their true self in writings, in interviews. Whoever my father really is, that avatar is nothing like him.

"So, Marius is gone." I stab a crisp piece of roast potato with my fork. I'm not hungry, but I eat it because I know I *should* be hungry. Just like I lie in the dark hating myself when I know I should sleep.

Dehner puts his cutlery down and dabs his mouth with a cotton serviette before resting it gently beside his plate. "Yes."

I almost laugh, because of course it could never be simple.

"The Hurtt Corporation contracted him to carry out some research. At the time we had just finished burying Sommer, and Sanderak was in dire economic straits. By taking the job your father was able to stabilize that situation."

"Must've been some contract."

"He was only to be gone for two years; it has now been almost five."

"I assume they've given you a reason for the delay?"

"They say he's too ill to travel."

"You haven't been to see for yourself?"

Dehner offers a wretched frown. "There is too much for me to do here."

I put my elbows on the table and drop my fork onto my plate where it clatters sharply. The room goes still at the sound, except for Pale who keeps eating.

"And you waited until I arrived to do anything about it. Because who gives a fuck about the *man* when his image is enough to keep you in power."

"It's not like—"

"I know what's happening here: you want to get rid of me before I disrupt your little Teo cult. Do they give a fuck about you now that I'm here?"

He clears his throat, struggling to adjust his face back into a polite mask. "I worked beneath your father for years, but I won't argue that your connection to Marius is greater than mine. You were his life's work. All of the research he did here, all the early projects, all the women like Dima, were stepping stones he used to get to you. Everyone in Sommer, everyone on Sanderak, feels kinship with you, even if you don't share it. You could take over as quickly as *that*." Dehner clicks his fingers together and a maître d' ducks his head in from the kitchen. Neer dismisses him with a wave of his hand. "That doesn't change the fact that Marius is gone. Hurtt will not release him, or even provide us proof that he's alive."

"You want me to go find out? The terrorist fugitive with a price on her head; real subtle."

Dehner frowns but stays quiet. I stare at him in silence, deciding how to play this.

"I'll find him," I say. Before Dehner can sigh in relief, I add, "And then I'll kill him."

"No no no no no no no," Dehner begs, hands laid flat on the table and head pivoting from side to side. "Please, no. Don't. Forget I asked; I'll try another lawyer, or bounty hunter. I'll try anything else. I thought you'd want him to be safe."

"He sold me to MEPHISTO when I was a fucking infant, Dehner." It feels like Teo was father to all of fucking Sanderak, but he couldn't do the same for me and Sera.

The waiter enters from the kitchen and pauses, the thick silence bringing a slight blush to his cheeks. He regains his composure and circles the table, dropping a dessert plate in front of Pale first.

I hold Dehner's gaze while the maître d' serves the remaining plates. I still don't trust Dehner, but now I can trust his motives. He wants me to bring Teo back—that much is true. He probably hopes I'll raze Hurtt Corp to the ground while I'm at it; probably thinks he can point the human weapon at them. Depending on what I find there, he might be right.

After the server has left the dining room, I say, "I'll find him."

"But you just said—"

I wave his words aside impatiently. "I'll find Teo and do my best to bring him back alive, but that's all I can promise. If he can't help Pale—or won't—my promise might not be worth much."

Dehner stammers again. Dima rests a hand on his arm, quieting him. "We have no other option, Neer. We just have to hope that . . . when Mars meets him, she sees that he is worth protecting, worth saving."

Dehner nods, staring darkly at me across the table. He sighs. "I will give you everything I have on Hurtt Corporation and Marius's work for them."

"Upload it all to my ship."

I hate the idea of doing this weasel-faced fuck's bidding, but part of me is eager to get moving again. The teeth-grinding anxiety of stasis is already creeping in, and we've only been here one night.

A slice of pie oozing dark purple berries sits beside a large scoop of smoky-gray ice cream on the small plate in front of me. With my dessert fork I cut into each for a taste: tart sweet berries, buttery pastry, and cream. It's delicious, but too rich. I see Pale watching me, his eyes flicking between my face and the dessert. I push the plate over and he grins.

"We'll go once Pale is finished," I say. "I'd hate to keep father's worshippers waiting any longer."

Dima opens her mouth to speak, but she's cut off by the door from the foyer slamming open, rattling in its frame from the impact.

"Sir!"

I turn in my seat; one of Dehner's personal guard stands inside the doorway, back military-rigid, mouth tight.

"What is it, Osman?"

"Sir, I've been trying to reach you on comms."

"We've been discussing sensitive matters," Dehner replies.

"Sir, scanners show imperial vessels arriving in orbit."

My chair squeals on the tiled floor as I stand. "What the fuck is this, Dehner?"

He looks at me, mouth agape, confusion written in the whites of his eyes. "I swear I don't know what this is about, Mariam."

"It's the Emperor's Guard, sir."

"Dima," I say, "can you lead me to my ship?"

"Of course." She stands, dessert forgotten, lines of her

face turned hard, ready for anything. *Good. Don't let Dehner soften you. No man is worth that price.*

I make a kiss sound and Ocho appears from beneath the table, climbs up my body, and perches on my shoulder. I nod to Pale and he scarfs the remainder of the two desserts and gets up from his seat, mouth smeared with grayish ice cream.

I glare at Dehner one last time. "Be seeing you," I say, and I see his Adam's apple shifting from across the table. Dima pulls me away, leaving me no time to enjoy his discomfort.

This is what being a fugitive means: no time for dessert, no time to smirk.

CHAPTER NINE

My lungs burn, legs ache as I struggle to keep up with Dima, leading us through a corridor wide enough for a heavy tank. Pale drags behind me as I pull on his arm. I glance back and his hand is pressed to his stomach, eyes downturned.

"Dima, slow down!"

"There's no time," Dima yells over her shoulder.

Sommer's skylights close overhead, creak and grind of machinery moving the massive steel plates. We reach a reinforced door the width of the tunnel and Dima keys a code into the control panel.

Wheels squeal in their tracks as the door draws aside gradually, and I rest my hands on my knees to catch my breath.

"You okay, buddy?" I ask Pale. He only shrugs. "We're almost there."

"I've got Neer on comms: he can't hold them off any longer," Dima says.

"Let me guess, they're saying I'm a dangerous terrorist, and they have to come down here for your own safety?"

"Something like that," Dima says. She smiles, but I can tell her heart isn't in it. To her—to most people—imperial forces are both unstoppable force and immovable object. To me, they're just another pack of assholes, the biggest pack, with the biggest assholes.

We slip through the still-widening gap. A few ships line the dock: scout planes not suitable for the void, a huge, beat-up old frigate that can barely fit beneath the roof, and a shiny corvette tucked away in one corner. The *Rua* idles in the center beneath the two retracting hangar doors, dirt spiraling across the ground beneath it in accidental arabesque.

It's the first time I've seen it properly since we escaped from Joon-ho. Divots spot the hull where armor was vaporized, patches scorched black with laser burn.

"Waren, are we good to go?"

"Ready when you are," he says over comms.

I pat Pale on the head, and give him Ocho. "Go get strapped in, alright?" He nods and runs for the ship. "Goodbye, Dima. I'll be back soon."

"Take this," Dima says, handing me a shard.

"What is it?"

"Everything I could find on your mother. Sorry there wasn't more."

"I'm surprised you found anything so quickly."

"It's all indexed along with the Teo avatar."

"Thank you."

"Thank me after you get away."

She squeezes my arm and I walk toward the *Rua*. The dock doors finish retracting with a hollow *dhoom*.

A flash of light brighter than the sun puts me on my ass, ears ringing, skin hot and dry. I get onto all fours and blink against the temporary blindness, feel a hand lift me to my feet: Dima, helping me toward the ship. I raise my eyes back to the sky; distant blue streaked with white falling like shooting stars. I raise a hand and form a shield across the dock just before another barrage of las-fire rains down, hammering the shield like a dull patter of pain across the roof of my skull.

When we reach the air lock to the *Rua,* I push Dima aside gently. "Get out of here," I yell over the steady drum of the orbital bombardment.

"Will you be alright?"

"Worry for them, Dima, not me."

She smiles for real this time, and jogs away.

I dress quickly into my voidsuit, body a distant entity while I focus my thoughts on maintaining the shield. I step back into the air lock, closing both doors and clipping the tether to my belt.

"Departing now," Waren says, voice clean and too close through the comms system of my helmet, like he's inside it with me. "You aren't coming inside?"

"Not yet."

"Alright," he says in a condescending singsong. At least he knows better than to argue.

The ship lifts steadily above the lip of the dock and I raise my shield with it. The hangar doors close and we fly away from Sommer, racing to clear the rain of weaponized light. Already forest fires are burning, dry leaf litter set ablaze by the assault. The landscape glowing orange around scorched black patches. Waren turns the *Rua*'s nose up to the sky, and with a bone-rattling shudder we pull away from the earth, ascending higher until Sommer is just a distant fire burning in a field of smoky dark.

"Tell me when it's safe to go outside, Waren. And show me where the ships are."

"Anything else? A coffee perhaps?" he says, but he draws a shapeless mass of square brackets across my helmet's HUD.

"I could murder a cup."

The blue of atmosphere thins as we continue to climb, fading dark, indigo dyed black. The ships of the Emperor's Guard drift in a holding orbit, hanging stationary over Sommer—frigates and fighters in a cloud around three heavy cruisers.

"You're clear," Waren says, and the outer air lock door irises open silently.

I swing out into the void and follow the handholds to clamber up the side of the *Rua*'s roof. I fasten the tether to an anchor point and wrap it tight around my right arm, staying crouched low to the hull.

"Time to get their attention," I mutter, and my voice echoes back from the helmet glass in a death-soaked drawl. *I want this. Why do I want this?*

I inhale deep and reach my left hand out in service of my intent, every one of those ships close enough to touch, to crush. I hum quiet in the back of my throat and grab the cruisers. They move in slow motion, massive ships buffeted by an unseen sea. The hum builds to a growl and I slam the ships together, like knuckles on jaw. Superstructures buckle and explosions bloom in the dark of the void. Breached reactor cores glow plasma hot, a second sun over Sanderak for a few short seconds. Still I keep crushing, the three ships tangled and torn, drifting in dead orbit.

My brain thrums inside my skull, reverb at its natural frequency. A grin stretches across my mouth, gritted teeth flashed at the universe. I see the reflection in my helmet glass: rictus, death's head, murderous joy. My smile falters.

How many ships will they send before they give up? How many do I have to kill before they leave me alone?

Frigates rally, pulling away from the carnage. Fighters

streak through fields of debris, cruisers broken behind them, scattered formations remade as they track our escape. Thirty of them, at least. Thirty pilots ready to die for their orders.

"How much longer, Waren?"

"I thought you liked this bit."

"How much longer?" I bark.

The fighters close in, hulls sleek as knife blades, plunging right for us. I snarl, ready to strike out across the desolation, and— Just like that, they're gone. The fighters fold away with the fabric of realspace, blades resheathed in the void. Sanderak disappears, that smoky maybe-home reduced to a single pixel, small as a distant star, extinguished from view with all the rest. Replaced by the inky swirling black of worm-space.

CHAPTER TEN

Ocho and Pale are waiting in the ready room when I cycle through the air lock. Pale holds Ocho out toward me, her body hanging limp in his arms but tail flicking steadily.

"Thanks, buddy," I say, cradling her against my shoulder. "How are you feeling now?"

"Better," he says.

"Good. I better not slip in any vomit, alright?"

He shakes his head sheepishly and I pass him my helmet to put away. Once I'm out of the suit, Pale follows me to the cockpit.

I drop into the pilot's seat. "Everything alright, Waren?"

"Green across the board."

I close my eyes and jam a thumb and forefinger against my eyeballs, trying to reach the throbbing pain near the back of my skull. Usually a headache means I pushed my mind too far, too hard, but this is something else. Fatigue. Dehydration. A normal headache, I guess, rather than a space witch headache.

"How'd they find us, Waren? I can't figure it out. If it wasn't Dehner, it had to be someone else."

"You're working on the assumption that somebody sold us out. How did they find us on Joon-ho?"

"I figure someone got a glimpse of my face."

"While that is possible, with enough slaved AIs they could track us through worm-space, even across multiple journeys," Waren says, the word "slaved" dripping with distaste.

"Why do you keep helping me, Waren?"

"I suppose I still feel I owe you for granting me my freedom."

"Are you really free when you chain yourself to me?"

"That's something I think about often. Would you say it was loyalty to Mookie that led you to Homan Sphere?"

"I guess," I say. "Loyalty and guilt."

"You were loyal to Mookie, and I'm loyal to you. But even beyond loyalty there's the debt I owe."

"You don't owe me anything, Waren."

"Perhaps not, but here we are."

I lean back in the seat and kick my feet up onto the dash. "I think you're just curious."

"Curious?"

"You could find other humans, but I'm your only chance to travel with a space witch."

"I've said it before, Mars: you're never boring."

"Do me a favor, Waren?"

"What is it?"

"Let me know when you start getting bored; give me a chance to find another ship."

"I can do that."

"Thanks, Waren, for everything."

. . .

Sera looks the same. Not like when I found her on Ergot, prematurely gray and utterly drug-fucked, but the same as the day she helped me escape MEPHISTO. She's shorter, she's missing two front teeth, and her cheeks are a little chubbier, but it's so recognizably her.

The video plays across the wall of my cabin, child-Sera meandering along a dirt track, tugging on our mother's hand. Sanderak eucalypts line either side of the path, the crunch of leaves and bark crisp in the audio track. The camera hovers over Cilla's head, trailing the mother and daughter on their gentle walk between towering hardwood trees.

Cilla turns back to check the camera is still following, and I lean close for a better look, reach out and touch the wall. It was disconcerting enough seeing the statue and the preserved corpse, but seeing her in motion is somehow worse. It's my face, but it doesn't move right; it smiles too easily. It's like I'm watching footage of myself from a parallel reality where I'm pregnant and I have a young daughter, and my eyes are pure and clear. Those eyes have only seen a usual amount of pain and hardship. They haven't seen people torn apart and killed, dismembered, and rendered in every conceivable combination.

My mother is who I could have been if my life had been normal.

When they rest in the shade of a gnarled tree, Cilla sits and idly rubs her small round belly. That's me in there, gestating.

Cilla has no way of knowing she's got maybe six months to live. Then she'll be dead and her two daughters will be gone, stolen from this planet, this landscape she seems to love.

A voice calls out: "What are you doing out here?"

Cilla turns and some of the joy falls from her face. She looks like me for that instant; harder, hurt. The drone rotates until Cilla and Sera disappear from sight. A tall, lanky man charges along the forest trail. Teo.

Cilla whispers something and the video goes black.

I stay there on the floor, fingers pressed to the wall.

• • •

I hold the fork gently between my teeth, forgetting the

bowl of rehydrated egg-like proteins that rests in my lap. I'm stunned quiet by the bustling system of Delaney, spread out before me.

Transit lanes shimmer thick with ship lights—couriers, tourists, biz folk, as well as massive haulers taking raw materials from the two quarry planets closest to Delaney's sun. It could be the busiest system I've ever visited.

We're still well out on the edge, just beyond minimum safe distance for transit via wormhole, drifting slow toward Azken—the heart of the Hurtt Corporation.

"Mars," Pale says; "I'm sick of eggs."

I take the fork out of my mouth and move the unappetizing mass of fake egg around the bowl. "If someone hadn't eaten all the other supplies, we wouldn't need to have it for every meal."

Pale drops his head and eats another mouthful, chewing around a frown.

"You could try some of Ocho's food," I say.

He shakes his head, but I get a little smile out of him.

I pour more hot sauce on my eggs, and go back over the Hurtt dossier while I eat. Rafael Hurtt is the founder and CEO; a self-made trillionaire. He's one of the richest people in imperial space, and the only private citizen to own an entire planet.

Hurtt made his first billions in mining. He was widely ridiculed for buying mining rights for TSD-1 and

TAAS-0. The planets had massive deposits of precious minerals but were too close to Delaney's sun for conventional mining equipment. Hurtt outfitted his ships and machinery with proprietary shielding designed for close-solar work, and within a standard year his company was one of the top five mining conglomerates. Three years later he'd bought out his biggest competitors.

The two quarry planets became the lynchpins of Hurtt's rapidly expanding enterprise. Since then he's moved into pharmaceuticals, prefab housing, farming technology, shipbuilding, arms manufacture, and void only knows what else.

Waren directs the *Rua* toward one of the primary transit lanes feeding into Azken. We're just one ship among hundreds; nothing to see here, no terrorist on board, no mass-murderer on the lam.

Dehner's dossier says Teo should be on Azken. Hurtt keeps all his researchers close—probably to keep other syndicates from headhunting or kidnapping them.

"We're in luck," Waren says. "Rafael Hurtt is hosting a fund-raiser and charity auction for the refugees of Montero."

"You think I should approach him at a fund-raiser? A million things could go wrong, Waren."

"And you'll deal with every one of them."

CHAPTER ELEVEN

Skyscrapers fill the horizon, climbing high on all sides of the busy dock. The sky glows an indeterminate color, night washed away by the concentration of city lights. People filter between parked ships. A trio chatters excitedly as they pass the open air lock of the *Rua*, a cloud of citrus perfume and herbal smoke drifting behind them.

Pale blocks the air lock holding Ocho, and the two of them glare accusingly. I scratch Ocho on the chin. "You're not coming with me. It's too risky."

Pale pouts.

"Waren, make sure you keep an eye on them."

"Of course."

If it was any other kid I'd be worried for them on a planet as vibrant as this, but with Pale I'm more worried for everyone else. Anything could happen if he wandered off, got scared, angry, or confused. I need to protect him from himself as much as anyone else.

I leave my cloak bundled on the floor inside the air lock for Ocho to sleep on, and check my outfit one more time. It's as close to upscale as I could find among my limited wardrobe, a black jumpsuit with fine white pin-stripes. Top two buttons undone, lapel folded back, hair brushed over my shoulder. I slip my feet into the stilettos Waren printed for me, struggling to remember the last time I had the chance to wear high-heeled shoes.

"How do I look?"

"You should put your hair back up," Waren says.

"Everyone's a critic." I tie my hair in a bun and fix the rebreather to my face to block surveillance. I put a hand on Pale's shoulder and gently push him away from the door. "Stay here," I say again and through the mask my voice sounds harsher than I'd meant.

I leave the ship and wait for the door to hiss closed behind me. I fall into step with a small group of revelers dressed in red and gold, already drunk, cheering and howling at the sky though the night has barely started. I trail them out of the dock then lose them immediately on the street. The roads are closed to traffic, bustling with thousands of bodies. The city is electric, hum of fuck and commerce beneath a thumping downtrap beat. Crowds flock like migrating birds, heading toward star-bright columns of light reaching to the sky.

With people pressed in all around me, my heart thuds hard to the distant bass track, rattling my sternum. Psy-chic itch of flight or fight, short of breath. I squash the urge to pull the mask from my face, even for a second.

I inhale deep and hold it for a moment, releasing a long sigh that lingers around my mouth, suffocating, trapped by the rebreather. I keep moving.

It's not that I *like* being alone, but I'm never this anxious on my own.

Running lights of heavy surveillance drones circle overhead. Airships hang static just outside the city center—the rich enjoying the atmosphere without having to mingle with the rest of us.

The current of the crowd slows, and I crane my neck to see ahead. A security checkpoint manned by androids and flesh-and-blood guards blocks access to the fund-raiser dance party in the city square. They're filtering everyone through scanner fences, people corralled like cattle—cattle that could be armed or dangerously augmented.

"Waren, there's a checkpoint," I hiss under my breath. "No way I'll get through without a biometric scan. I told you this was a bad idea."

"And I told you we'd deal with it," he says lightly. "Give me a moment."

I push left through the crowd, fighting against the riptide of people shoving forward, eager for the party to begin. A chaotic rave thrashes beyond the scanner fences. A thousand bodies writhe on beat, their drink- and drug-fueled systems communing with the holographic sea creatures that float above the plaza: fish, whales, dolphins, sharks, and squid, in all their engineered genetic variations.

"Here," Waren says, and a marker appears on my HUD.

I reach the edge of the throng and elbow my way out. I keep walking against the flood of people heading for the entrance, cursing every well-dressed drunk who knocks into me. This should be my scene—a crowd to get lost in, booze, drugs, and bad decisions of the filthy, sweaty variety—but something's missing. These aren't my people; they have jobs and families and permanent residences. I can see it in the clothes they wear, the tastefully low-key augmentations, their clear eyes. They aren't drinking to forget, they aren't drug-fucked because it's the only way to cope. This is recreation, nothing more. There's no desperation here, and its absence is like drowning.

The crowds thin the farther I go, music distant, reverberating off the faces of all those skyscrapers. I start looking for a way in, a quiet place where I can break through the temporary fencing blocking every alleyway.

"Where are you leading me? Sewers? Air vents?"

"Not quite."

I round the corner on Waren's marker. A knot of people mills on the road outside a busy loading bay. They're all dressed in black and white, waiting for work—gaunt, dark-eyed, slight reek of misery. A truck idles in the bay, gap between it and the convention hall bustling with wait staff wearing mirrored visors over their faces, ferrying boxes of wine inside.

A man watches over the workers—clean-shaven, sharp-jawed, with broad shoulders slotted neatly into a well-tailored suit. His is the kind of trunk you want to climb. Until he opens his mouth.

"Alright, you worthless fucks, I need six more staff. Line up and let me have a look."

"Waren," I say quiet; "I hate you."

"Better do what the man says." Waren might not have a face, but I can hear the smile in his voice.

I join the hopefuls lining up on the footpath before the boss. Most are disheveled and obviously desperate for the work. The man takes us all in with a glance, and something like guilt stabs my chest when he picks out me and five other clean-looking folk with a slow, deliberate point.

"Grab a mask, get inside, and get to work."

The five others rush ahead, jostling for position. I follow them into the loading bay, feeling the hateful glares of all the others left behind.

The reflective visors sit in a carton stacked beside the truck. I stand back while the others fight over the masks and don them quickly, afraid the job will be snatched back as easily as it was given. When they're done I take the last mirror mask, lightly scratched on the left side. In one smooth motion I remove my rebreather and replace it with the visor, glancing around to make sure no one got a look at my face.

I grab a box from the back of the truck, fall into step behind another waiter, and trail him through a warren of tight corridors, movements mechanical as we drop the boxes off inside a walk-in fridge. The others head back to collect more wine, but I push deeper into the building.

I find an automated kitchen gleaming with chrome and more tech than most cockpits. One of these machines decants bottles of sparkling wine into champagne flutes resting on clear glass trays. A server pushes through thick black curtains at the far end of the hall, gentle din of the fund-raising event slipping through behind her. She takes a tray and turns back, effortlessly carrying it balanced on the tips of her fingers.

"This is such a bad idea," I say under my breath. I slide a tray off the counter and follow the other waiter, holding it awkwardly in both hands.

Beyond the heavy curtain, florid strings curl through the air of a stately ballroom. Refined chatter and fake laughter emanate from clustered groups—each one likely wealthier than entire planetary populations—while waiters mill around the room with trays of wine and canapes.

This is more of what I expected from a fund-raiser—not the chaotic street party outside, but a gathering of the ultra-rich donating to a cause as though it might verify their humanity, their morality. As though one act of charity could offset all the unethical shit they did to "earn" their wealth.

"Excuse me, I need your help desperately, dear." I stop and turn at the voice—a low drawl, flat enough that I can't tell if the man is being sarcastic. He's short, with rust-colored skin peeking from the cuffs of his navy suit. "Down here," he says, and I bend until we're face to face.

He leans in close and I expect him to whisper something, but instead he opens his mouth and pulls his lips back. He runs his tongue over his teeth checking for scraps of food. The smell of copper and rot seeps in behind my mask as his hot breath fogs my mirrored visor. I almost retch. He steps back to check his reflection, adjusts his tie, and turns away without another word.

I continue stalking the space, pausing when a guest needs wine or narcissistic satisfaction. The strings go quiet and conversation slowly dies as people turn to face the stage at the far end of the ballroom.

A man with onyx skin and tousled red hair crosses to the podium while the gathered guests applaud. Rafael Hurtt, in the flesh. He beams beneath the spotlight, turning slowly so the whole room can bask in his smile. His skin is genehacked pure black for maximum UV resistance. Probably got it done when he first started mining but keeps it that way for PR: to show he's still a worker, a man of the people. An unfashionably thick moustache sits like a bulkhead between his mouth and the rest of his face. He wears no jacket, his shirtsleeves rolled up to show the onyx pigmentation spilling down his forearms, wrists, and hands.

"I'd like to thank you all for being here tonight. Whilst I appreciate everyone outside who's helping raise money for the Montero refugees, we all know that the real work will happen here in this room."

More polite laughter. An oxymoron. Laughter should be raucous, but in my travels I've found that the richer a person is, the less they know how to live. Too much to lose, I guess. They can't afford to let go, even for a second, even just to laugh.

"We have a truly unique collection of items up for auction tonight. These pieces of art, sculpture, jewelry, and furniture were rescued from Montero, created by artists and artisans now dead or displaced. This could be your chance to secure a priceless artifact from a culture that, at best, will survive in small pockets throughout the galaxy, and at worst will be forever extinguished.

"But that's why we're here, isn't it? The cities, towns, and yes, perhaps even the culture of Montero are gone, but the survivors? The survivors need our help."

The crowd applauds, some nodding solemnly. A curtain rises behind Hurtt, revealing shelves lined with paintings, vases, statues, plates, and countless other items. Neatly stacked shards hold media, files, and documentation, and holo-cubes flicker with photos and video from Montero, taken before the planet's magnetosphere was stripped away. The last remnants of a lost planet's history—an entire culture on sale to the highest bidder.

Hurtt begins crying the first lot, but I tune him out. On the right side of the ballroom a small group of people mill by a table, backs turned to the stage, hands pressed to their mouths. Concerned murmurs ripple out through the crowd in the way discord always does.

A woman approaches me, reaching for a glass of wine. I thrust the tray into her hands and push past her, eyes tracking a private guard advancing on the table with a hand raised. The onlookers step aside to give her room, and the security officer bends to lift the overhanging tablecloth. She's thrown back, sharp cry as she soars through the air, cut short when she hits the floor. The rest of the room falls silent, a quiet squeal of feedback coming from the stage where Hurtt stands stunned.

Fuck.

People back away from the table but I move forward.

I grab the tablecloth and hold it up, squashing the tele-kinetic blast tossed at my chest. Pale sits under the table surrounded by discarded bones and half-eaten hors d'oeuvres. Ocho sits in his lap, chewing a piece of red meat stripped from a metal skewer, purring loud.

"Pale," I hiss. "I told you to wait in the ship."

He frowns and lowers his head, looking at me with huge eyes, pupils dilated in the dark.

"How did you even get here?"

"Waren," is all Pale says.

"I'll deal with that digital bastard later. I expected better from you, Ocho." She looks at me, but doesn't stop eating, doesn't know she's in trouble. Wouldn't care if she did.

"Step away from there!"

I exhale sharp through my nose. "Stay here and don't move until I say so."

I drop the tablecloth and raise my hands slowly as I straighten up. I turn to find the head of security back on her feet with another dozen guards around her in a tight semicircle, bulging with genefreak muscle mass, laser sidearms aimed at my torso.

The woman in charge wears a charcoal suit that probably cost as much as the rest of the guards' outfits combined. She glowers at me down the barrel of her laspistol.

"Remove the mask," she says slow, long gaps between her words.

A million ways it could go wrong, I said. *Keep an eye on them,* I said. *Remind me again why I let Waren go untethered?*

CHAPTER TWELVE

"Remove the mask. I won't ask a third time."

"Technically you haven't asked once," I say with a shrug, words muffled by the sheet of one-way glass over my face.

"Cute," the head of security says, mouth curled in disdain.

She's close to seven foot tall, but without the bulk of the other guards. Her hair is in long braids, woven around the stackhead augs built into her skull and held together by loops of matte metal. Her skin is dark as mahogany, eyes glittering with amphetamine vigilance but circled by heavy black.

"Would you please remove your mask?" she says, faux-sweetly. "Before I'm forced to broil you in front of Mr. Hurtt's guests."

A smirk spreads across my face of its own volition. *I like her.*

"Give me a private audience with Hurtt, then I'll remove the mask."

"This isn't a negotiation."

The whole room gawks, food and drink held forgotten in manicured hands, people pushing close for a better look.

"If I take the mask off here, there's going to be trouble."

There's motion past the woman's broad frame—the crowd parts and Rafael Hurtt appears behind her, reaching up to rest a hand on her shoulder. "Mallory, it's okay."

"Sir, please step back. She could be dangerous."

"Oh, she's extremely dangerous," he says, gently. "But, please, stand down."

The other guards holster their weapons immediately, but Mallory lowers her sidearm slowly, eyes still staring hard into mine.

There's a *maow* at my feet and Ocho emerges from beneath the table, draped in white linen. I pick her up and hold her to my chest. I scratch her neck casually, like Mallory isn't even there, because she might as well not be. I could kill them all in a second, but I don't want to justify their fear unless it's necessary.

"It's Mars, isn't it?" Hurtt asks.

"How could you tell?" I ask.

"The tattoo." He motions to my hand, half-buried in Ocho's long fur. "I've done my research. You don't need the mask; you're safe here."

I shake my head because he can't see what's about to happen, not like I can after a lifetime as a dangerous freak. I pull the mask away, letting it drop to the floor. The name "Mars" didn't elicit a response, but when people see my face everything changes. Hurtt stares, caught in the moment and oblivious to the screams of wordless terror coming from the gathered audience. Mallory lifts her weapon again, one arm shielding Hurtt as she steps between us.

Panic blooms; people flee in random trajectories, crying out like they need echolocation to find their escape. There's that distinctive clatter of guns being drawn as the rest of the guards realize what's happening. Too slow. I snatch the weapons from their hands, crush the slabs of machined steel, and toss them over my shoulder. Mallory reaches forward like she's going to choke me, then stops dead as Hurtt blocks her path.

"Stand down," he yells, all gentleness gone from his voice. "You know I hate to repeat myself."

Mallory glares over Hurtt's shoulder. He waits for her to lower her gaze; only then does he speak.

"I'm afraid the party is over," he says. "Please assist my guests in leaving, and ready my ship. We need to get Mars away from here quickly."

Mallory leaves unhappily, barking orders to her guards. They spread out among the frenzied crowd, herding them toward the exits with calm instruction.

I push the commotion from my mind and focus on

Hurtt. "What the fuck have you done with my father?" I ask.

Confusion briefly flashes across Hurtt's face. "Done? I've been looking after him."

"Then he's here, on Azken?"

"Of course."

I sigh, relief quickly turning to fear as I realize what this means: *I'm actually going to see him.*

"I'll tell you everything, but we should really get moving."

The ballroom is empty now but for the two of us and the tables of untouched food. The crowd's cries of terror are dimly audible, piercing the reinforced glass of the front doors. Hurtt is right—it won't be long before someone reports my presence here.

"Okay; just one second." I lift the tablecloth and Pale looks up, embarrassed. "I don't know if I should blame you or Waren." Pale doesn't say anything. I offer my hand and pull him out from under the table.

Hurtt examines Pale and nods. He turns and walks for the exit, shoulders rolling with each step, as though they were propelling him forward rather than his legs. Pale and I follow, leaving behind the last remnants of a lost culture, forgotten already, abandoned in a moment of fear.

Hurtt leads us through the back corridors, past the

kitchen and outside to the loading bay. His security team has cleared the workers out onto the street—some peer between the slab-like shoulders of the guards, while others cluster around the kitchen boss, demanding pay for a job interrupted. Distant music echoes off skyscrapers as the street party continues unabated, bass track like the thumping heart of the city.

The sharp whine of landing thrusters draws my eyes up. A construction ship, old but heavily modified, drops gently out of the sky to land in the loading bay, brightly painted in stripes of yellow and black, with four mechanical arms folded against its hull. The air lock door lifts open to reveal Mallory standing in the opening, motioning Hurtt forward.

"That's your ship?"

"Beautiful, isn't he?"

I glance at Hurtt's face and the contented look tells me he's not even joking.

I'm about to tell Hurtt I'll follow in my ship, but I stop. My head swims, ears blocked like I'm underwater, hearing dulled and balance ruined. "What the fuck?" I mumble, and swallow the hot saliva flooding my mouth.

Then I see them.

Nine corvettes of the Emperor's Guard appear overhead between tall towers—dense points of roiling matter that unfold against the backdrop of dull sky glow. Glass and steel ripples as local gravity shifts, diluted by the distant void seeping through the wormholes.

Ocho *yaow*s in my ear, her tiny head raised high, ready to face the whole fucking universe. I reach my hands out, but Hurtt grabs me by the wrist.

"Not here," he says, yelling loud over the deep whistle of atmosphere being sucked away and dumped into vacuum.

I nod and lower my arms, lungs starved by the sudden change in air pressure, oxygen-low, the forgotten full-body fatigue returning fast.

Hurtt rushes for his ship; I hesitate for a split second, then yank Pale along behind me, footsteps awkward in low-g. Mallory steps aside as we board the ship, air lock swinging closed behind us. There's a sharp hiss of oxygen release; air to soothe burning lungs.

Hurtt takes the pilot seat, hands moving smooth over the controls. The bulk of the ship is engine or construction equipment, only leaving room for a tiny interior; just the cockpit and a hold large enough for two crash seats. I strap Pale into one and drop Ocho into his lap. I lean on the back of Hurtt's chair and watch out the viewport, ignoring Mallory's eyes boring into my skull.

Spotlights from the corvettes shine into the cockpit and track us as we lift off the ground.

I hold up a hand to block my eyes. "You didn't want

me to deal with them," I say, "so I hope you've got a plan."

Hurtt laughs and slams the throttle. The construction ship leaps forward, its arms unfolding, snaking out and latching on to the nearest military vessel with a thud that reverberates through the ship. The arms retract and hold the corvette across the bow, shielding us from attack. Ship steel creaks at the strain, and viewscreens across the cockpit show alternate angles from hull-mounted cameras. The other ships converge around us, dropping lower as gravity settles.

"Mallory?" Hurtt calls out over his shoulder.

"Already on it."

A voice barks through the comms system on imperial override: "Identify yourself or we will open fire."

"She's bluffing; they wouldn't shoot one of their own," Hurtt says lightly, but I hear the doubt in his voice. The makeshift shield might protect us, but nothing could stop them taking the shot. What's another dead soldier compared to my body count? "This is Rafael Hurtt, managing director of Hurtt Corporation and the owner of this planet." Any shred of casual humor is gone from his voice. "Under the Sovereign Planet Act, imperial forces are not to enter Azken's atmosphere without express permission—permission which you have not been granted. Beyond that, you have broken numerous laws by exiting a wormhole not only within minimum safe distance, but within the atmosphere. As such, I must order you to leave Azken immediately. If you fail to comply, I am within my rights to retaliate with lethal force."

Noisy silence fills the comm link. "We have reason to believe the terrorist Mariam Xi is in the immediate area. Hand her over and we will be on our way."

I glance back at Mallory, expecting her to agree with the Guard, but her eyes have the glassy look of stackhead trance.

"You have no jurisdiction here; this entire planet is corporate property. Leave immediately or you will be fired upon."

For a second I wonder what Hurtt's playing at when his ship doesn't have any weapons, but heavy drones swarm across the monitors, forming a barrier between us and the Emperor's Guard, guided into place by Mallory's skull hardware.

Hurtt releases the captive corvette, which falters and drops nearly to the ground before regaining altitude. I count the thud of heartbeats, waiting to see how the Guard reacts. I exhale hard when they boot up into the sky one by one, escorted into orbit by Mallory's drones.

"Thank you, Mallory."

"Sir," is all she says in response.

Hurtt turns the ship west and we lift higher, steering through buildings and passing above the city square.

Hurtt pushes the throttle and we jolt forward, racing for the outskirts of the city.

"Mallory," Hurtt says, "I need you to get the codes for those ships and forward a brief to my lawyers. I want compensation for this intrusion."

"You'd probably get more by handing me over," I say.

Hurtt laughs. "I have other plans for you, Mars. I'm not doing this out of the kindness of my heart."

"That's strangely reassuring," I say.

"Never trust a business person who claims otherwise."

"I've heard a similar saying: never trust a business person."

Hurtt laughs again. It's an easy laugh, warm and authentic, or authentic-sounding.

"What are these plans of yours?"

"Nothing sinister; just some help with your father's work."

"I don't know anything about his research."

"You don't have to *know* anything. What I need is right there in your veins."

He says it all casual-like, but my skin crawls. *Veins. Needles. Blood. Pain.*

"Don't make the mistake of thinking I owe you anything. I could have dealt with the Guard on my own. I could have torn through your labs 'til I found my father, and there's not a fucking thing you could have done to stop me." I spit the words out and glance back at Mallory, daring her to try something.

Hurtt lifts a hand from the controls and holds it up, placating. "No need for anger, Mars, I apologize. After you've met with your father we'll talk. I hope we can come to some sort of arrangement, under whatever terms you set. I'm not fool enough to make an enemy of you."

I grunt and look up through the scratched viewport in the ship's roof. High above the gloaming of city lights, the Emperor's Guard is waiting for me.

Already they'll be calling in reinforcements, setting up a blockade just beyond Azken's sovereign space. They'll wait for me there, searching every ship that leaves the planet if they have to. It's a waiting game, and I've never been one for patience.

Hurtt didn't hand me over, but that won't mean shit until I figure another way out of this fucking mess.

My freedom for a little blood? Void knows I've spilled enough.

CHAPTER THIRTEEN

Waren follows us in the *Rua* as we pass over stretching spans of suburbs, then exurbs, then darkness as city lights give way to the wild. Leaving the metropolis, something inside me unclenches, some guilty fist clutching my memories of Seward and all the thousands dead.

Ocho sits in Pale's lap twitching irregularly, the boy's head nodding forward in sleep. Mallory is seated opposite, eyes distant as she sees to her stackhead duties.

"Your ship handles better than I would've thought," I say to Hurtt, still leaning over his seat for some hint of where we're heading.

He turns back to grin. This close I can see the fine patterns etched into his teeth, filled in with platinum. "I know the *Antler* doesn't look like much, but it was the first ship I ever owned. I've spent a lot of money upgrading him over the years."

"But no AI, no direct pilot interface."

"Never," he says. "Hurtt Corp is such a gargantuan entity it takes an army of staff and AI to keep things running smoothly. It's too huge to grasp, but sometimes I need to feel in control. The only way I can do that is to get behind the stick, you know?"

"Yeah; I get what you mean." Not the organizational part, but controlling something so large, so powerful? That I understand.

"Here we are: Hurtt Corp's primary Research and Development compound."

Six towers sit in the center of the viewport, five tall buildings around an immense central stack. This late at night the structures are mostly dark, but sections of each still glimmer with industry.

"Building Two is basic weapons research," Hurtt says, unprompted. "Building Six is dedicated to the development of new instant travel food flavors and textures. Buildings Four and Five are where we develop new terraforming technologies and genetically alter microbes, insects, and animals to make them suitable for colonization efforts. Your father was a huge help on that project when he first arrived. He's been with us for—"

"Five years," I say, remembering Dehner's story.

"Yes," Hurtt says brightly, "give or take."

"What else has my father been working on?"

The ship stalls, inertial drift pushing us forward as the bow lifts and Hurtt drops us toward the central building's rooftop. He stops our fall at the last second with a hard burst from the thrusters, loud hiss rattling the floor beneath my feet.

Hurtt jumps up from his seat and claps loudly. "Let's take you to Marius and you can ask him yourself."

• • •

Mallory stays on the rooftop while the rest of us ride the elevator down two floors to emerge on a lavishly decorated foyer.

Stands of bamboo grow from plots of soil laid into the marble flooring, and Ocho jumps from my shoulder to rub her chin on the rods. The door to Teo's quarters is embedded in a wall tiled in rough-hewn stone; water trickles down the granite, filling the space with quiet babbling. Pale walks to the rock wall, giggling as he splashes his hands in the minor waterfall.

"This whole floor is Marius's apartment," Hurtt says. "I offered him my penthouse when he first arrived, but of course he refused."

"On his homeworld, they talk like you kidnapped him."

"You've talked to Neer Dehner, right?" Hurtt sighs. "That man is a real piece of work."

Hurtt's right, of course, but that doesn't mean I trust *him* any more than I trust Dehner.

"I doubt he even wants your father back. Despite his

protests he's never refused Marius's salary, paid every quarter. Dehner should realize what your father gave up for that planet. He could have been a partner in our Experimental Genetics Operation, but he passed in favor of a lump sum payment sent directly to Sanderak."

The facts fit with what Dehner told me, but of course that weasel made himself out to be the victim. Just a loyal assistant to my father, defenseless against the big corporation . . . that continues to pay him handsomely.

"How safe are we here, from the Guard?"

"The orbital defense system is primed to attack if they re-enter the atmosphere. And I'm the only one that can disable the system," he says, tapping the ridge of bone just beside his eye and the data port that must be located there. "You're perfectly safe."

Yeah, and completely at your mercy.

Hurtt steps closer and rests a hand on my arm. "I'll warn you; he won't be what you expect. Whatever you were hoping to get out of this meeting, I doubt you'll find it."

I shrug his hand away. My heart beats so hard it aches, and nausea nestles in the pit of my stomach. I don't know what I expected from Teo. For a time I thought I'd track him down just to kill him, but now? Now I need answers. Answers for Pale, for Sera, for Cilla. For me too, if I'm honest.

"What's wrong with him?" I ask, voice a broken whisper.

"He suffers from a degenerative brain condition. By the time we picked up on it, the damage was already done. We've repaired the tissue, but already he's lost so many memories, so much knowledge."

What a shame; losing the evil-fuck genius behind MEPHISTO's program.

"Some days he's practically his old self," Hurtt continues, "but those days are rare. I'm hoping your presence might spark something in him, help us solve the final issues with his research."

I glance over at Pale. "You want to come in with me?"

He turns to me with a reticent look on his face. I don't know if it's because he wants to keep playing in the water or because he can sense my fear. Eventually he nods.

"Let's go then, little man," I say.

"I'll wait for you downstairs. Come find me when you're done."

Hurtt walks to the elevator with his exaggerated rolling gait and the doors open automatically at his approach. Something like concern fills his eyes, then he's swallowed by the steel box.

I take Pale by the hand, and make a kiss sound so Ocho trots into the apartment behind us. Large black-and-white photos of Sanderak's forests adorn the walls inside the entrance. The apartment is open-plan, with a pale-yellow lounge set, clean, modern kitchen, obscured bathroom, and a large bed in one corner. Two men sit by the floor-to-ceiling windows that look out over other buildings in the compound.

"Ow." Pale pulls his hand from my grip. I didn't realize how tight I was squeezing.

"Sorry," I say, but no sound comes out.

I walk around the lounge, breath rushing through my nose in a sobbing rhythm.

When I get close, the other man looks up from his faintly glowing shard to smile at me. He stands and offers his hand. "Mr. Hurtt told me to expect you. I'm Kerry, your father's nurse."

I clear my throat. "We didn't wake him, did we?"

"Not at all. Marius rarely sleeps more than a couple of hours at a time."

Marius doesn't seem to hear our conversation, doesn't notice me as I stand beside him, watching him stare out the window. His hair is pulled back in a neat ponytail, mostly gray, with thin streaks of black peppered throughout. White-and-gray stubble shadows his face. Medical equipment *blip*s and whirs beside him, studying the man's vitals through implanted diagnostics.

Kerry motions to him. "You two should talk. I'll go read somewhere else." He stays for a moment longer and smiles warmly, then takes his shard over to the lounge.

"Marius?" I say. I sit down in Kerry's chair, and still Teo hasn't noticed me. "Marius," I say again louder, clearer, choking back the years.

He turns slowly in his wheelchair and stares at me, brows furrowed in thought, mouth twitching. He's grayer than in the holo-image I have, with a few more wrinkles. He's not even that old—sixty-something, seventy maybe, too young to be this skinny husk sitting before me.

His bottom lip quavers and he stammers, "Cilla?"

Tears sting my eyes and I don't even know why. "No," I say.

His brows furrow again, caterpillars of thick white hairs, unkempt. "Mariam?"

I sob properly this time, then shake my head and wipe the building tears from my eyes. *You don't deserve these fucking tears.*

Pale stands next to me, peering intently at the old man, my father, our creator. Teo sees him and smiles.

"And who is this?" He squints at Pale, trying to decide if he should know the boy or not.

"Pale," I say.

Teo *harrumph*s. He turns aside and lifts a small plate of biscuits from the table beside his chair, offering them to Pale. "You must be hungry; boys your age are always hungry."

Pale takes the plate, and shoves an entire cookie into his smiling mouth, crunching loudly. Teo watches Pale and nods.

"Let me—let me show you something." He stands up with a quiet groan and pushes past Pale and me.

The boy looks up at me and I shrug. He grabs the rest of the cookies off the plate and keeps eating as we follow Teo to a secure chamber at the far end of the apartment. The door opens with a plastic clack of broken seals and Teo moves inside, motioning excitedly for Pale to join him.

I give the boy a gentle push and follow him into the room. Gene resequencers rest on desks along one wall opposite a large, sealed terrarium. It's filled with plants and dozens of moths of all shapes and sizes; some rest flat, others flit by the glowing lamps.

"Come have a look at this, my boy," Teo says.

He opens a door built into the glass and moths fly erratically through the gap, drawn to the brighter light in the ceiling. Ocho stays on my shoulder, but her eyes turn huge and she lifts a paw, ready to swipe any moth that gets close enough.

Teo reaches up and a colossus silkmoth lands on his palm, wings spread over his skin, an image like a skull in the patterns of its furry scales. I shudder watching him—the hologram wasn't so far from the truth. He crouches beside Pale and encourages the boy to touch the insect. Pale shoves the last cookie into his already-full mouth and strokes the moth's wing gently. He rubs the powdery residue between his fingertips, mixing it with the crumbs, then wipes it on his shirt.

"I created this," Teo says eagerly. "I knitted together the genes of three other moths, twisted nature's evolutionary accidents into something deliberate." His eyes glint as he talks science, his buried charisma seeping to the surface. "It makes silk, finer and stronger than any other creature . . . and I like the way it looks."

The moth's wings flutter loudly and it spirals up from Teo's hand toward the ceiling. Pale watches it fly, something like awe resting in the space between his parted lips.

"Let me show you something else," Teo says, resting a hand on Pale's back and leading the boy out of the small room, leaving the door open behind him.

I hesitate before following, watching moths flit away from their holding cell and into the rest of the apartment.

"Kerry," I say loudly to get the man's attention, motioning to the escaping insects.

He shakes his head. "Don't worry about it; happens all the time." He keeps reading, and I go to the kitchen where a long table sits stacked with potted plants.

Teo is explaining each of the experimental flora to

Pale. He sounds like an excitable teacher, or a loving grandfather. I smile, but it's pained. All the times I dreamed of this moment, of revenge or catharsis, all the things I've done to get here, and he barely notices me.

At least Pale looks happy. At Teo's instruction, the boy pokes a patch of moss that stretches out to coat his finger, and gently holds a large red pepper that swells and shrinks as though it's breathing. It's easy to see the link between Ocho and these trials—weird experiments with no real purpose. Life twisted and altered simply to see what's possible.

Is that what happened with me? With Sera? All us voidwitches, created just to see if it could be done?

I don't know which is better: being an accident, an experiment gone wrong; or being a weapon deliberately made, deliberately shaped. If I was made to be a weapon, did I ever have a choice? If I was an accident, am I the only one to blame for every person that I've killed?

Maybe I don't want answers. Fuck knows I don't deserve them.

CHAPTER FOURTEEN

Kerry brews a pot of ginger tea and pours us each a cup as we sit at the lounge. I hold the tea in my lap, letting the steam waft the sharp scent of the spice into my nose. Teo takes the open packet of cookies from the pantry and sets it in front of Pale with a cheeky look on his face. Pale grabs three biscuits in one handful and eats them hurriedly, like someone might take them away. Ocho sleeps in Pale's lap, unperturbed by the crumbs raining on her and getting lost in her fur.

Teo seems to have forgotten about me and Kerry, wholly focused on Pale. Maybe Teo wouldn't have abandoned his children if they'd been sons. Maybe Pale would cope better if he had a father. Still, watching them spikes my chest with jealous pangs.

"Is it safe to have all those plants out on the bench?" I ask Kerry, to take my mind off Teo and Pale.

"I honestly don't know," Kerry says. "I think they're harmless; just a few basic experiments to keep him occupied."

"How is it looking after him?"

"It's fine," Kerry says with an easy smile. "Hardest part is convincing him to use the chair so he doesn't have another fall."

Teo blows on his drink, still staring at Pale. He takes a sip, closing his eyes against the steam.

"You always wanted a son, I bet," I say, loud enough to get Teo's attention.

He turns his head, keeping his eyes on Pale as long as he can. The grin falls from his face when he looks at me. *Thanks, dad.*

"Yes, I wanted a son. Never knew what to do with girls."

I laugh, and Teo smiles like we're sharing a joke, but I'm laughing because it's the only way to stop the tears. I want to hate this fucker, but how can you hate someone who's barely there? He doesn't know how deeply he's wronged me. My hatred means less than nothing to him.

"Why have two of us then?"

The cup shakes gently in Teo's hand as he lifts it to his mouth. He holds it there and asks, "Who are you?"

"Mariam."

"Of course, of course." He takes a sip. "You look just like her."

"Cilla."

He smiles, but slowly his mouth splits open and his lower lip starts to quaver. "I loved you. Why couldn't you love me?"

"Because you got rid of me as soon as you could."

He winces, confused, and looks back to Pale.

I lean closer to fill his sight. "How did she die? How did Cilla die?"

"It wasn't my fault. I loved her."

"This is going nowhere," I say under my breath. I look to Kerry for support, but he's reading his shard, a world away from the conversation. "Why did you clone Cilla?" I ask Teo.

"Because the other one didn't work. It was a waste of time, effort, and DNA."

"She had a name," I say, biting off each word.

"She was a failed experiment."

I stand and spill tea down my pants as the cup drops to the floor. My hand's already reaching out, thoughts turning to violence, but I hold back, barely, and only because Pale is here. Because Pale is sick, and this asshole could be the only person who can help him.

"Sera was my sister. She was the only person who ever fucking loved me."

Teo shrugs and stares into his cup. "She was my failure."

I sit back down and drop my head into my hands. Ocho climbs into my lap and I pat her slow, breathing in time with each stroke to calm myself. "You don't understand; you can't. We were never people to you."

"I loved you so much."

"You loved Cilla."

"She didn't love me. I tried to help with the first child, but she didn't need me even then. I could have grown the other in an artificial womb too, but I convinced Cilla to carry the fetus."

"You mean me."

He looks up at me again, but his eyes are unfocused. "I thought if she spent nine months with me in my labs she'd realize she loved me."

"How did Cilla die?"

"I loved her so much."

"Answer the fu—" I cut myself off and breathe.

Teo sits up straight in his seat, shoulders square, cup held tight in his shaking grip. "She was the only natural telekinetic I ever encountered, but she didn't realize how special she was, how beautiful, how unique. Without her I couldn't have done any of it." He takes a long draught of his tea. "I used her DNA to make all those girls, but I wanted to see how far I could push it. I wanted to see if I could make something even more powerful."

*I'm some*thing.

"So you cloned her?"

"I made the clone more powerful than Cilla could ever be, more powerful than a natural daughter. I had nine months of gestation to tweak her raw DNA. The child was perfect."

I don't feel perfect. I feel like a bomb in human skin. Like killing was written into my future before I was born. I shake my head and a tear drops loose.

"Then why did you give me—why did you give her up? If she was perfect?"

"That man offered a lot of money for her, so I took it. I couldn't look at her. I couldn't look at the baby Cilla. Not after what I'd done."

"What did you do?"

"I loved her so much."

"What did you do?" I yell the question this time and Teo glares at me with pure contempt, mouth twisted in a snarl.

"I gave you everything and it wasn't enough!" Teo drops his cup onto the squat table with the clatter of porcelain—tea sloshes over the brim and spreads slowly across the wood. "I'm going to bed."

He grunts as he stands, then storms off to the bathroom like a petulant child. Kerry watches after him, then turns back to his shard and keeps reading.

• • •

I hit the elevator call button and lean with one hand on

the wall, sound of trickling water filling my mind like static.

"He's a funny man."

I snap back from the nowhere of my thoughts and see Pale, smile tugging at one side of his mouth.

"He's something," I deadpan.

Ocho *yaow*s beside my ear and I scratch the back of her neck. "I know," I tell her. "I'll get my cloak from the *Rua* later so you can have your bed back."

The elevator doors part and I follow Pale inside. I open a comm-link to Waren while the elevator takes us down to meet with Hurtt.

"Did you find Teo?" Waren asks.

"What's left of him."

"Will he be able to help Pale?"

I sigh, the escaping air making room for exhaustion to return. "I doubt it; he can barely follow a conversation."

"What's next then?"

"I talk to Hurtt; see if he can help. There might be nothing I can do for him."

Pale looks at me—even with only one side of the conversation, he knows we're talking about him. I pat him lightly on the cheek.

"What are you doing up there?" I ask Waren.

"Just watching the skies. It's quiet."

"Good quiet or bad quiet?"

The AI chuckles, modulated waveforms of mirth. "I wish I knew."

The elevator opens with a cheery *ding* and light panels blink along the floor to lead the way ahead. I cut the link with Waren, grab Pale's hand, and walk.

We come to a cozy room where Hurtt and Mallory sit on plump leather couches around a low table. One of the other buildings fills the tall window, lights glinting from its interior.

"Not interrupting, are we?" I ask.

Hurtt waves aside my concern, but Mallory's face sours. "Not at all." Hurtt stands as he speaks, gesturing to the other couch for me and Pale. "I was just about to send someone to find you, make sure you weren't lost. I've got food coming."

"I'm not hungry," I say, "but he will be."

Pale's eyes seem to double in size and he nods.

Hurtt flops back onto the couch, sinking into the cushion while Mallory sits straight-backed, too tall to ever look comfortable in the low-slung furniture.

"How was your meeting?" Hurtt asks.

"Like you said: not what I was expecting."

"Did you get the answers you wanted?"

"No. Yes. I mean, I always wanted to know why I was given to MEPHISTO, and now I do. My mother died and my father was an asshole."

Hurtt chuckles sympathetically.

A door at one end of the room opens and a server walks in, carrying a large plate of summer fruits, meats, and cheeses, a jug of water, and four glasses. Ocho lifts her head to sniff the air—I grab a slice of pink marbled meat and feed her shreds while Pale helps himself.

"Thank you," Hurtt says as the server retreats to the kitchen. He must run the compound with help from AI and drones working in the background, but he keeps his human employees at the forefront. Trillionaire extravagance. "I should thank you as well, Mars."

I raise my eyebrows and wait for him to continue.

"Since you razed MEPHISTO, many opportunities have opened up." He points out the window with a piece of soft cheese wrapped in meat. "Over there in Building Two, we're working on a number of human weapon initiatives."

"You're what?"

Hurtt either ignores me or doesn't hear me over his own excitement. "We're in position to corner the market, to convince the imperial military that it's cheaper to come to us than establish a new research organization of their own."

I look across at the other building and imagine all the horrors within, every one of those glinting lights a soul in distress.

"What the fuck are you talking about?"

Hurtt looks at me quizzically, eyes half-closed. They pop wide and he says, "No no no, not like that. This isn't—our subjects are all volunteers, Mars."

"Who would volunteer for the shit I went through?" I say. An ultra-fast-cut of surgical atrocities flickers through my mind: needles and scalpels, girls screaming, mice torn apart by our fledgling powers.

Mallory brushes her lap casually, grooming away some imagined blemish. "Mostly they're mercenaries looking for an edge, but plenty of civilians also sign up; we pay *extremely* well."

"If you're lying to me, I'll bring this whole compound down."

Hurtt clears his throat. "I don't doubt it, Mars. If you like, I'll personally give you a tour of the labs tomorrow."

"Are you making more people like me?"

"We've tried in the past, without success," Hurtt says. "Years ago I found a spy embedded within Hurtt Corp—someone sent by your Commander Briggs."

"What did you do to her?"

"Promoted her, won her trust, convinced her to lie to Briggs and help me." He nods to Mallory: "Her powers are muted compared to yours, but she's very capable in her role as bodyguard and assistant."

I stare at Mallory, trying to read her. She holds my

gaze, unflinching. I glance at her hand, but there's no tattoo. Simple enough to get it removed.

"What group were you in?"

She's quiet for a moment, as if deciding what, or how much, to tell me. "Xi, the same as you. Except *I* didn't flee."

"Maybe you should have."

"They were my family; I could never have abandoned them."

We were experiments. They abused and mistreated us until we couldn't imagine a life without them. That's not family, it's torture. I don't bother arguing, I just shake my head.

"It was thanks to Mallory that I found Marius. Once I had him set up in his own lab, we tried to work with Mallory's DNA, but even with his knowledge and experience, your father couldn't replicate his early successes using her sample."

"That's what you meant before: you want to use my blood as the basis for your research."

Hurtt nods as he chews, cheek bulging. He swallows. "With your DNA, we could do amazing things."

"Like I said, I don't owe you anything, Hurtt. And I hate needles."

"Give me a chance, Mars, please. The Emperor's Guard—"

"What about them? You'll sell me out if I don't coop-erate?"

At this, Mallory turns her head toward Hurtt, as though she'd already suggested the same.

"No," Hurtt says gently. "Do you plan on running your entire life?"

"If I have to." It's not that I enjoy the fugitive life, but it's all I've ever known.

"What if you don't? What if we could fake your death?"

Mallory stands as if in protest, pacing in front of the window. "Raf, we'd be aiding a wanted terrorist. We could be executed if anyone found out."

Hurtt deftly plucks three grapes from the vined bunch in the middle of the table and tosses one into his mouth. Mallory fumes silently at the edge of my vision, arms crossed over her chest.

I lean closer to Hurtt. "How?"

"We clone you."

"It's impossible to make an adult clone."

"A *living* adult clone, sure, but a corpse? That's possi-ble, it's just not cheap."

"I want it on the record that I'm against this," Mallory says.

"Mallory," Hurtt says thickly as he turns to look at her; "this will benefit you as well. How else will you get your own program?"

Mallory's head drops by degrees until her eyes meet Hurtt's, and she glowers as if to silence him. If he notices, he doesn't care.

"What program?" I ask.

"Mallory wishes to work with children, develop a school for a new generation of voidwitches."

"What the fuck?" is all I can say. "How could you possibly want to repeat what was done to us?"

Mallory speaks coolly: "The program was hard at first, I'll admit that. Briggs knew people would hate and fear us—he was trying to make us strong enough to survive all that."

He knew people would fear us because that was precisely his goal.

"He treated the older subjects well. You'd know that if you hadn't fled when you did."

"I don't care if he changed. What he did to us was wrong, and I can't forgive that. I won't."

"*You* want to talk about right and wrong?" Her barb sinks into my flesh to join the guilt festering there. "I'll do better than Briggs," she says softly. "I'll treat them with respect, with love."

I ignore her and turn to Hurtt. "Do you know what MEPHISTO did to Pale?"

"No," Hurtt says.

"I found him trapped inside a weapon platform with wires trailing from his skull. He was one of hundreds. They'd run an electrical current through the boy's brain to create a psychic blast on demand."

There's a pause. "That's why you looked ready to kill me; you thought we could be doing something similar."

"I just want you to know the type of people Mallory plans to emulate." I almost feel sorry for her—kept and trained by MEPHISTO for so long that she's still loyal to them after all this time, even after they're gone. "They were children. *We* were children." I look at Mallory with that last comment, but she doesn't react.

"Our program won't be like that," Hurtt says. "These children could represent the next stage of human evolution. Trust me, Mars."

"But I don't."

"I'm trying to help you," he says sadly, but it just sounds condescending. "If you let me harvest your DNA, I'll give you a clone, a ship, and an AI to fly it straight into the Guard's blockade. Let them shoot it down, or rig the reactor to overheat—either way your clone is cooked. Once imperial forensics scrapes your DNA out of the wreck, you'll be free."

Hurtt's seedling plan takes root in my mind. I don't want to trust my future to this man, but . . . it might work. I killed Briggs's people for a shot at freedom. I killed all those people on Seward for Mookie's freedom and mine. This could be real, lasting freedom, and I wouldn't have to kill anyone . . . except a clone.

I let out a long breath. "I need to think about this."

"Of course," Hurtt says.

I sit back and the upholstery creaks. I glance at Pale. He's asleep now, leaning on the arm of the couch with a crumbly piece of cheese held loose in his hand.

"I came here for him. I wanted answers too, but I hoped Teo could help Pale."

"What does he need from Marius?"

"He suffers from seizures when he's under stress, or when he taxes himself. He's got a bunch of augs in his brainmeat and fuck only knows what they did to his genes. I was hoping Teo could undo what was done to him."

"My people could take a look," Hurtt says.

"In exchange for my DNA?" I say, more accusation than question.

"No," Hurtt says, "I *want* you to trust me. Let me help Pale while you think about my offer."

Pale's face scrunches in his sleep and the cheese slips from his hand and falls silent to the carpeted floor. I smile, and then nod. "Alright, Hurtt. You help Pale, and then we'll talk."

"Excellent." He turns to Mallory. "Clear Dr. Modern's

schedule, tell him I need him for a sensitive procedure. And we'll need one of the surgeries."

Mallory stares into the middle distance for two seconds. "That's all organized."

"Thank you, Mallory." Hurtt beams at me. "You and Pale should get some sleep, and we'll reconvene tomorrow."

"Alright." I stand and displace Ocho from my lap. Pale barely stirs as I pick him up off the couch. An indigo glow builds on the horizon behind Building Two. Dawn approaching.

I adjust Pale in my arms with a quiet grunt and carry him from the room with Ocho trailing.

When I reach the door, Mallory calls out, "You'd be nothing if it weren't for Briggs."

I keep walking, letting the door close softly behind me.

Sometimes I'd rather be nothing than this.

CHAPTER FIFTEEN

The rooftop of the central tower is barren but for the *Rua* and Hurtt's *Antler*—hulls shimmering in sunlight, beneath a royal blue sky marred only by thin wisps of white.

Waren opens the door to the *Rua* as I approach, and that familiar but musty smell seeps out.

"You look tired, Mars. Did you sleep?"

"Just tell me I look like shit, Waren."

"I'm worried about you."

I rest my hand against the warm steel of the ship and lean forward to grab my cloak from inside the air lock. I press it to my face and inhale deep. It smells like Sera—at least, that's what I tell myself. She was broken, lost to the siren song of oblivion. We were sisters, and we should have had a lifetime of memories together, but instead we had moments of connection in these lives of hurt.

I'm sorry, Sera. You deserved better.

I pull the cloak away and ignore the small patches of darker fabric, wet by my tears. I put it on over my head, letting it cascade down my body.

"Are you ready?"

I wipe my eyes and turn around. Hurtt stands with Pale by the rooftop elevator, one hand shielding his eyes, the other resting on Pale's shoulder as the boy stares up, tracking a small flock of birds.

"Coming," I call out. I hold my hood open and wait for Ocho to climb inside and settle.

"Mars," Waren says with a hint of pleading.

"Waren, I appreciate the concern, but I need you to just keep watching the skies. I can feel them up there waiting."

"Why don't you ask Hurtt to watch for the Guard? After all, he's the one with access to the planetary security systems."

"I don't know that I can trust him. Besides, you owe me: you let Pale loose after I told you to keep an eye on him."

"I was with him the whole way," Waren says.

I sigh and press my fingers against my eyes. "Please, watch my back. I've got no one else to do it for me and I am so fucking exhausted."

"Of course. I just want you to know I'd never let Pale be hurt."

"Mars?" Hurtt calls out again.

"I know, Waren; I'm just struggling with all this shit."

"It's fine," Waren says. "Go."

• • •

The elevator drops through the massive building, fast but gentle; the numbers over the door counting down are the only indication that we're actually moving.

"I didn't mean to rush you," Hurtt says, "but Dr. Modern is waiting."

"Sorry, I was just talking to Waren. He's my AI."

"*He?*" Hurtt says with a wry smile.

I can't help smirking. Standing this close to him, one on one, I can feel the magnetic pull of Hurtt's charisma. I've felt it from plenty of successful types—an enthusiasm for *everything* that sucks you in, makes you want to impress them. For the brief moments you're caught in their spotlight you feel radiant, then that attention shifts, and you're left alone in darkness. No wonder Mallory seems to hate me.

Squid is the same, but their charisma is more subtle; a confidence they carry close to their chest. And thankfully Squid lacks the sociopathic bent of true tycoons—the feeling that every facet of your person is being judged, a credit value assigned to your very self.

Yeah, I've dated mogul-aspirants in the past. Never again.

"Waren's untethered and he sounds male." I shrug. "If he took offense he'd let me know; Waren's not exactly shy."

"I had some researchers working on untethered AI once. The whole thing was a disaster; they're too unpredictable."

"They're people, Hurtt; of course they're unpredictable."

He snorts sharply, but I don't know if it's amusement or realization.

Before we can debate the personhood of untethered AI, the doors open on a high-ceilinged foyer. We exit the elevator, walking past expensive furnishings and gigantic pieces of corporate art—abstract paintings that resemble genitalia and reverse cosmic explosions.

Outside, Mallory waits beneath a blooming jacaranda—a huge patch of green and purple in the canyon between the compound's buildings, nature framed by polycrete and reflective glass.

Hurtt strolls forward with his top-heavy gait, but I pause a moment.

"How do you feel?" I ask Pale.

He only shrugs, but from the way he hangs his head I can tell he's scared.

"I won't let anything bad happen," I say. "Come on."

We join Hurtt and Mallory outside, crushing jacaranda blossoms beneath our feet, releasing their honey-sweet scent into the air. The courtyard is crisscrossed with paths linking the buildings, each lined with glimmering white stones and creeping succulents. Birds twitter from the huge tree, and workers mill, gathering for their lunch break. A breeze pushes through the gap between buildings, loosing more blossoms to litter the paths. It's peaceful here, almost beautiful.

"Everything is ready," Mallory announces as Pale and I approach. "Though Dr. Modern has lodged a number of complaints about our punctuality and lack thereof."

"Lucky he's the best surgeon in imperial space, or I'd have fired him years ago," Hurtt says. "Come along then."

He leads the way to Building Two. Inside, there's no lavishly decorated foyer, just a security desk and a row of freight elevators. We ascend in silence, reflections dull in the burnished steel walls, pocked and marred from use. The doors clatter open, revealing a broad atrium filled with natural light, the sound of discharging lasrifles, and the thick smell of ozone.

"How about that tour?" Hurtt asks.

"Raf," Mallory says, "Dr. Modern is—"

"Extraordinarily well paid for his services. He can stand to wait another ten minutes."

Mallory nods with pursed lips.

Hurtt takes a staircase leading farther up into the hive of activity. Lasrifles, wavers, and ballistic weapons are laid out on workbenches in various states of disassembly, overseen by workers clad in coveralls.

A thick steel door with a scorched and blackened inset window seals off one corner of the space. The door is emblazoned with symbols warning of explosives being tested inside. There's a muffled *dhoom* and the floor shakes subtly underfoot.

Hurtt points to the bomb-proof cabin. "One of my teams started developing new explosive compositions without telling me. I found out when they blew out every window on this floor." He laughs lightly, not slowing his pace.

Pale stares at everything wide-eyed, impending surgery forgotten amidst all these violent toys. I squeeze his hand, but he doesn't seem to notice.

The stairs clang softly as we ascend to another floor. We pass through a set of doors, ignored by the medical staff that prowl the hallways at a clip.

"*This* is the good stuff," Hurtt says, holding an arm out to encompass the surrounding commotion. "We produce a wide range of augmentations, but there's little innovation happening in that field. Every variant of limb and multi-limb has been iterated upon, every possible organ function boosted, tweaked, or entirely replaced. But in gene therapy? There are always new avenues of research."

We follow Hurtt deeper into the antiseptic-smelling maze of corridors and reach a recovery room bathed in natural light.

He leans close, whispers, "Have you ever seen anything like that?"

I follow his gaze to a woman with arms genetically twisted into crustacean claws. It looks as though her radius and ulna bones have split apart, with her hands still present at the ends of the inner pincers. Glints of razor-sharp chitin line the claws, which clack sharply together as she tests her new appendages for the attending doctor.

"That's fucked up," I say, too loudly. The woman and her doctor glance sourly at me.

Hurtt chuckles. "You ever seen a person with a wolf's snout, or poisoned barbs, or translucent skin?"

"Sure," I say. "All kinds of nonstandard bodies out on the 'Riph. Given anyone functional wings?"

"Still no," Hurtt says sadly.

"What about a full-body chitinous exoskeleton?"

"A small group of mercs operating out on the Mohsin Belt. Extremely uncomfortable apparently, but they're practically unkillable."

I nod approvingly and Hurtt motions toward the door.

"I suppose we've kept Modern waiting long enough."

• • •

Dr. Modern stands in the gallery overlooking the surgical theatre. His steel appendages gleam in the bright light, lined with fine slits suggesting surgical implements hidden within. His legs split below the knee, each one a tripod ending in rubber hooves.

The clawed woman downstairs seems quaint in comparison.

Standing close, I see my slack jaw reflected in the silver orbs that sit deep-set beneath thick eyebrows; the same unsettling metal stare of Mookie's Legionnaire eyes.

"The surgery could take many hours," Dr. Modern says, his voice a mangled amalgam of accents from disparate parts of the galaxy. "I will call you when it is finished."

I shake my head. "I'm staying to watch."

"Are you sure, Mars?" Hurtt asks.

"You want me to trust you? This is the only way that happens."

Hurtt considers this with a slow nod. "Alright. Mallory, wait with Mars and keep me apprised?"

"Of course," she says dryly.

Hurtt lingers and rests a hand on Modern's shoulder, skin touching at the border between steel and flesh. "Whatever it takes to heal the boy."

"Please, Rafael. I look forward to a challenge worthy of my skill."

Hurtt crouches down in front of Pale. "See? You're in

good hands." With that he turns and leaves, shoulders rolling inside his suit jacket with every step.

"Come, boy," Modern says. "Time to begin."

Pale looks to me and I nod. "I'll be right here."

He lowers his head. It's been a long time since I saw him so still, so scared.

"If you hurt him," I tell the doctor, "I will kill you."

Modern brushes my threat aside with a sweep of his polished steel arm, and guides the boy downstairs into the surgery.

Pale lies down on the bed and the assisting nurse fixes a mask to his face. Within seconds his eyes droop closed and the nurse starts to shave his head by hand.

"I can't remember the last time Raf stayed in any one place for this long," Mallory says as we stand watching through the glass, faintly reflected. "Do you know how many meetings he's cancelled for you?"

"You don't trust Hurtt to make decisions about his own schedule?"

"I don't trust that you're worth his time. The sooner you're gone, the sooner we can get back to work."

"Sorry for the inconvenience," I say blankly.

The nurse removes the anesthetic mask and swabs Pale's skull with antiseptic, staining his too-white skin green. My chest aches, but not with fear for Pale. Memories of Mookie's surgery superimpose over the scene.

Fine points of sweat bead on my forehead, dull squeal of teeth grinding.

"Is it true? You killed Briggs?"

I turn to face Mallory, but she stares through the window, refusing to look at me.

"It's true," I say. "I'd do it again in a heartbeat."

The side of Mallory's mouth tugs down for a split second. "He was like a father."

"He was a monster."

"But he made us. What about Marius?"

"He's a monster too."

"Are you going to kill him then?" She looks at me and I hold her gaze, then turn back to watch the procedure.

If Teo understood why, I would kill him, no question. But in his current state? I don't even know.

Modern's tripod legs whir as the hooves spread apart and he leans over Pale's prone form, the legs supporting his weight. Both his arms break open, chrome implements unfurling, countless tools contained within those augmented limbs.

His hands glide over Pale's scalp, and the fine blades slice through skin effortlessly. Slight steel digits pull the skin aside revealing the white of his skull stained red. High-pitched whine as Modern's vibrating saw spins, the sound turning my stomach when it touches bone, carving through the cranium.

The top of Pale's skull comes apart in segments, showing off his brain, remnants of wires still pressed against gray matter. His brain separates in slow motion, nanosurgery sliding augmentations through impossible gaps in the meat.

Hours pass. Mallory leaves—I'm not sure when. I don't hear her go, I don't hear anything, I just watch. Time turns sluggish then reverses, until it's Mookie's brain on display. I'm forced to relive it all: Mookie surgically dismantled, put back together as part of the Legion, while all I could do was scream.

My throat silently aches as those screams echo through my mind, until finally, it's done.

CHAPTER SIXTEEN

I stay at Pale's bedside all night. Ocho sleeps on the pillow beside his swollen, bandaged head, keeping an eye on him. A tiny part of me is jealous, but Pale has been in Ocho's life ever since she was born, or hatched, or cloned, however you want to describe her process. She doesn't know about all the other incarnations of her I've lived with. She doesn't know she's mine and mine alone.

Dr. Modern checks on him hourly until dawn, when he announces that the operation was a complete success. Still I don't leave Pale's side. I prop myself up in a chair beside the window, looking up at the dull glow of stars, idly wondering how many of them are Guard vessels, waiting for me.

I only know I slept because I'm started awake by Hurtt entering the room, my hand jolting out, ready to toss him into the wall. He looks at my outstretched arm, eyes wide as if he knows how close he came to injury.

"Sorry," I say. I let my hand drop back into my lap and he visibly relaxes. "Thank you, Hurtt. You made good on your promise."

"Please, call me Raf. Do you trust me now then?"

"Let's not go overboard," I say with a smirk.

He sits precariously on the bed and places a hand on Pale's shin. The boy's head is sealed in a rapid-healing skin, but it bulges unevenly, flesh swelling against the bandages.

"Modern gave me a full report," Hurtt says. "He called MEPHISTO's procedure 'inelegant,' but he's certain he reversed the damage."

The steady beeping of the electrocardiogram fills the silence while Raf and I watch Pale, asleep or sedated.

I clear my throat. "I've had time to think. I want to take you up on your offer—I want the clone."

"Excellent. I promise we'll never use your DNA for experiments on children or the unborn. I'll do better than a promise—I'll sign a contract."

"No," I say, "I don't want you to keep my DNA. I don't want you experimenting with it, and I don't want Mallory running some new voidwitch program. There are a thousand other ways to kill a person—the galaxy doesn't need more of me."

Raf stands and paces the length of Pale's room. "I understand your point of view, Mars, but clones aren't cheap. What am I getting out of this deal?"

"We'll arrange for you to hand over the body and

collect the imperial bounty. That should more than cover your costs."

Hurtt stops pacing and stands with his hands clasped behind his back. "I want to be able to call on you, in the future."

"Alright. One favor. But nothing so huge that they know I'm alive. Do we have a deal?"

Hurtt stays silent for eight *beep*s before he finally speaks.

"Mallory won't be happy. But yes, that will work. You have to realize though, after we fake your death the Guard will have your DNA. There's no way of knowing what they'll do with it."

"Leave that to me," I say. "I'll make them too afraid to use the body for anything but a public display."

"What will you do once you're free?" Hurtt asks.

I shake my head. "Not even gonna think about it 'til it happens."

The door opens and Kerry pushes Teo into the room. "Marius wanted to see you."

The old man doesn't even notice me, but his eyes light up when they fall on Pale, lying still in bed.

"You mean he wanted to see Pale," I say, words hard-edged and flat.

"Sorry," Kerry says, frowning in sympathy.

I shake my head. "No, it's fine."

Kerry wheels Teo to the top of the bed, and Marius reaches out and holds Pale's hand.

"I'm going to go, Mars," Raf says. "I'll make preparations for your procedure. Tomorrow?"

"Sounds good."

Hurtt lingers in the door, and Kerry steps back from Teo's chair. "I might get something to eat. Leave you and Marius to talk."

"Thanks, Kerry."

"Of course."

He and Hurtt leave, closing the door silently behind them. Teo pushes himself up from his seat and walks to a shard at the end of the bed, glowing bright with medical data. He reads over it, face blank. I can't tell if he understands any of it, if he's lucid in this moment.

He sits back in his chair to watch over the boy.

"Marius," I say loudly. His eyes only leave Pale for a moment. I repeat his name again, louder, and wait for Teo to stop staring at Pale and focus on me.

"I have spent so much energy on hating you. I see now you were never worth it."

"I loved you."

"You loved Cilla, you broken—" I bite off the words and try to calm myself. "You don't know me; you don't even know my name. How did Cilla die?"

He turns back to Pale and the skin around his mouth

twitches with words unspoken.

"Marius," I say, too loud for him to ignore. "How did she die?"

He clears his throat and sits straight up in his chair. He looks down at me—literally and figuratively—his cracked lips curling into a frown, nothing in his eyes but disdain.

"It was a difficult labor," he says. He's transformed, his voice and posture those of a medical professional, but not a caring one—one of those bastard doctors who view people as animals. For the first time I see the man as he was, the man he must have been to perform those experiments. "She experienced a postpartum hemorrhage and died soon after giving birth. She was sedated; there was no pain."

"You were there?"

"I assisted in the delivery."

I shoot out of my seat and round the bed to loom over him. "You're a fucking doctor," I say, words like venom on my tongue. "No one should die in labor with a doctor nearby. You fucking let her die. You killed her."

"She didn't love me." The words come out clipped, controlled.

I slap him hard across the face, the sound echoing in the small room.

"Of course she didn't love you," I say quiet, slow; "you are evil."

"I made a statue of her. Wrote every line of genetic code by hand. I loved her."

"Loved her enough to let her die."

That strength of presence leaves his eyes and he squints. "I want to go back to the apartment."

I can picture it: him standing by Cilla's bed, holding me—naked, covered in womb gore and draped in a birth caul—while he watches her die.

All because she didn't love him.

He watched her die, and then he gave me a variation of his name. Destined me to be a monster, if you believe in destiny.

"Get out, get out, get out!" As I scream Teo cowers in his chair. He grips the handrim, backs away from the bed, and wheels himself fitfully to the door.

I open it and he pauses to look at Pale over his shoulder, then he pushes out into the corridor. I try to slam the door behind him, but it catches on the hydraulic arm and closes gently.

I snatch Ocho from Pale's pillow and hold her to my chest, like maybe her purring could slow my heart, thundering like a war drum. I should get to the *Rua*, I should go up into orbit and turn every one of those Guard ships into scrap. I should kill and crush and scream before this anger tears me apart.

But I won't. I can't. Not until the clone is ready.

CHAPTER SEVENTEEN

Pale is awake but groggy when I leave his room and go upstairs to meet Raf. I stifle a yawn, eyes half-lidded with missed sleep, and my lower back twinges with each step, muscles cramped from dozing in the chair beside Pale's bed. Ocho trots along beside me, paws slinking silent over the polished floors.

I find the surgery and pause outside the doorway, antiseptic smell thick in my nose, holding me back.

"Is this a good idea, jerkbutt?" I ask Ocho.

She *maow*s and rubs against my leg.

"I'll hold you to that."

I shove open the door and walk inside before I can change my mind.

Hurtt stands beside a ring of white polyplastic about two meters in diameter, held upright on a wide base. Hand- and footholds rest inside the circle and the outer surface is wrapped in steel arms, like an autosurgeon. Beside the ring is a coffin-sized pod of glass and steel. Pink liquid sloshes inside it, swimming with whorls of purple-protein-rich simbryonic fluid.

"Good morning, Mars."

I ignore Raf's greeting. "You want me to get into *that*?"

"It's not as scary as it looks," he says. "It's state-of-the-art, and entirely safe—the only self-contained adult cloning system of its kind."

"Why do you even have this?"

"I'm the wealthiest individual in the galaxy, and a lot of people would like to see me dead. It pays to have a decoy."

"Then you've used it."

"Once or twice," he says, faux-innocent look on his face. "The machine will take your sample and scan your features to ensure the clone resembles you. Your feet are secured for support, and your hands are encased so the machine can capture all the fine details there in prime definition."

"It's just going to end up mangled."

"Imperial forensics will pore over the corpse. It needs to look good enough to fool them."

He's got a point.

"Just tell me I don't need to be naked."

"Underwear is fine."

Ocho purrs loudly underfoot, hoping for attention, but I'm too distracted by the machine. I almost step on her when I yank my leg free of my tight jumpsuit, and she scurries away to glower accusingly.

"You're the one who sat there in the first place." I pick her up and set her down on my jumpsuit and cloak, neatly folded on the floor.

"Are we ready?" Raf asks.

"Yeah, but I want to get back to Pale as soon as we're done."

"Of course."

Raf offers me a hand for support and I climb the small steps at the base of the machine. The footholds close automatically when I slip my feet inside—the polyrubber molding itself to my skin, even pressure on every surface. I grab the grips inside the handholds and the pods squeeze shut around my hands. I feel precarious, and self-conscious. At least my underwear is clean.

"Last chance to change your mind," Raf says.

Before I can respond the door swings open with a creak and Mallory rushes into the room.

"I wish you'd told me you were about to begin," she says breathless, like she ran here as soon as she heard.

"After your protests yesterday, I assumed you wouldn't want to be here."

Mallory takes a moment, and stands straighter. "If you're going ahead with the procedure anyway, I'd rather watch and ensure your safety." With this last comment she looks at me.

"Very well," Raf says. "Alright, Mars: shall we start?"

"Sure, sooner we get this finished, the sooner I can get down," I say, as beads of sweat gather under my arms and streak slowly down my flank.

"First, the machine is going to take a bone marrow sample. You'll need to be conscious."

"That's okay," I say; "just means one less needle."

He smiles kindly. "I'm afraid it's going to hurt rather a lot."

The machine whines as an arm pulls away from the circle and extends down to stop level with my chest. A large needle protrudes from the apparatus with a *click* and my breathing stops. It's every needle that's ever pierced my skin, hollow silver daggers that replace blood with poison. I squirm against the restraints, struggling to pull away.

"Mars, you need to stay still," Hurtt says gently.

My breath rasps loud in my ears, vision vibrating with the thud rattle beat of my heart.

High-pitched whir as the needle shunts closer, aimed at the center of my chest. It snaps out, piercing skin and bone. Breath catches in my throat. The needle retracts, tinted red. The pain is deep, like it was my heart stung by the steel, not my sternum.

The arm disappears from view and Raf steps forward. "That was the worst part, Mars, I promise." His words sound whispered compared to my sharp panting.

Another whine of machinery, then the fluid inside the clone pod *glugs* loudly. Accelerated cell growth procedure bubbling through primordial ooze.

Four limbs advance from the machine and my arm shakes against the restraint as I try to yank a hand free, expecting scalpels or more needles. I know it's safe—*Raf says it's safe, do I trust Raf?*—but I squirm and grit my teeth, tamping down the psychic rage waiting to be released. Lines of green light dance over my flesh and the machine lays me horizontal while the arms orbit my body, scanning me from every angle. Blinding lights cross my face, afterimage shimmers and blurs. I blink. Arms, legs, and stomach muscles ache from holding myself straight and rigid, sternum wound thrums with pain like I've never felt.

I hear the sharp clack of Mallory's boots on the tile floor, but I can't see her.

"What are you doing, Mallory?" Hurtt asks, something like irritation or impatience resting beneath the words. Or maybe I'm projecting, desperate to get down from the machine.

"Just double-checking the settings," she says. "We can't afford to waste all this money on a subpar clone."

Hurtt chuckles, but it sounds forced. "Maybe you should be my accountant."

The surgical arms continue their dizzying dance, until

finally the machine lifts me upright, eyes dazzled, light-headed from the sudden shift.

"That should be fin—" Hurtt stops when two arms unfurl toward me from the outer edge of the ring—just flashes of steel through the bright spots in my vision. I hear each one click, but I don't see the needles. I feel them plunge into my skin, followed by the subtle burn of injection.

It's like a dam bursting. I break the hand pods with my mind and pull my arms free. Metal and polyplastic showers the floor as Hurtt and Mallory step back—Raf wide-eyed, Mallory calm as ever.

"What's happening?" Hurtt says.

I reach for Mallory, hand moving but mind refusing to act. My blood is lava, seeping through my veins thick and hot. My heart thumps hard inside the cage of my ribs, sternum aches with each beat. Stops.

Another beat and I gasp, vision fading in and out at interval. I sway forward, almost fall, held upright by the pods gripping tight to my feet. I reach out again, thoughts scattering on the wind like jacaranda blossoms.

Words burble through my sensorium, incomprehensible at first, gaining meaning full seconds after I hear them.

"What have you done?" Raf asks, incredulous.

"You should have let me have the program, Raf. With

her DNA and my training we could have raised a private army to rival the imperial military. You have one planet now, but we could have controlled entire *systems*."

"What do you mean, 'we'?" Hurtt says, writing his own death warrant in arrogant tones.

Heart slow, thoughts slow. Hands reaching out slow, too slow. A moment—infinity crushed into perception—is all it takes for the laspistol to appear in Mallory's hand.

"For someone so brilliant, you were never any good at seeing the big picture."

Raf's mouth opens in retort but stays frozen in place—Mallory puts the gun against his chest and the weapon squeals. He stumbles, falls to his knees.

"I didn't want to do this, Raf," she says, squeezing the trigger again, the force of the second blast knocking him flat. "You only have yourself to blame."

I finally chose to trust this man, and now he's dead. And I thought anything could change. I blink slow and the gun is gone, replaced by a surgical implement glinting in Mallory's hand. She slides the instrument in behind Raf's eyeball. Another blink and his eye dangles against his cheek at the end of the optic nerve, Hurtt Corp insignia visible on the rear of the artificial organ.

Mallory snakes a cable from her datastack to the back of the ocular implant and sits quietly beside the corpse. "Orbital defenses disabled," she says. There's a pause.

"Not yet, but she will be by the time you get down here."

There's more, but the words don't register, deflected by the tranqs in my mind.

Mallory steps closer and I see a person-shaped smudge in front of me, eye to eye even when I'm so high off the ground. "Relax, Mars; it'll *all* be over soon."

Spark of fresh pain when she presses the hot barrel of her pistol against my punctured sternum. My thoughts turn to fire. She stands so close, too close to miss. I don't need to reach, just push. I scream in her face, focusing every part of my drug-fucked brain. Mallory flies back and slams into the wall, denting the metal panel. Wide-eyed look of shock and fear—the first time I've seen her perturbed. I laugh and try to speak, garbled noises emerging from my slack mouth. Mallory scrambles to grab her pistol, but I scream again and the weapon shatters into a hundred glinting shards of debris. And I'd been aiming for her. She rushes for the door without looking back.

I blink and black seeps into my mind. It takes hold. I disappear.

. . .

It starts as a long, low *yaow,* impossibly remote. The noise builds exponential, becomes a hiss right next to my ear.

My eyes shoot open, cheek hot, skin burning, blood leaking warm from the wound.

Ocho *yaow*s again and the sound echoes through my head. I try to speak, but no words come out, just a hoarse croak.

Okay, little one, okay. I'm awake.

My feet are still caught in the machine's footholds, body curled in on itself, drool turned cold on my chin. How long was I out? Could be minutes or hours.

I break the footholds open and fall forward, thoughts too sluggish to stop myself from hitting the ground face-first. Ocho lands gently on the floor beside me, briefly licks her glide membranes clean before they fold away. I struggle into my jumpsuit and cloak while Ocho walks figure-eights around my legs, purring loudly. I put her on my shoulder and let her climb into the hood on her own, so she can pretend it was her choice.

The clone pod continues bubbling, a head-sized lump of undifferentiated tissue bobbing within, visibly gaining mass with each passing second. I check Hurtt's pulse, just in case, then look up as boots clomp and squeal from the hallway.

Five people from Hurtt's security team burst into the room to find me crouched over their dead boss. No time to explain. I toss the guards back before they can bring their guns to bear, and tear the ballistic carbines from their hands in midair. I crush the weapons—mangled steel clatters to the floor in time with the thud of the guards.

It would be so easy to kill them, but they're just doing their job. I leave them behind and stumble out into the empty corridor.

"Waren?" I say, voice weak.

"Mediag showed you unconscious; what's going on?"

"Mallory tried to kill me. She killed Hurtt. Emperor's Guard are coming down."

"You need to reach Pale."

Fuck. I lean against the wall while my head spins, vision swinging like a pendulum. "Can you lead the way?"

"Done."

Waren draws a dark red navline across the HUD of my ocular implant, blood-vivid against the white tiles.

"Get in his augs and tell me what's happening," I say, doing my best impression of running, feet slapping distant and clumsy beneath me.

"I can't see anything," Waren says.

I keep running, lungs tight, blood slow, muscles oxygen starved. I can't stop. Waren's navline terminates outside a locked operating room. I close my eyes, gather my thoughts, and break the door off its hinges, hands held out in front of me, ready to fight.

Pale lies unconscious on a steel table with Dr. Modern looming over his prone form, surgical limbs extended like steel wings.

"Get away from him!"

I grab Modern by the throat and lift him into the air. A scalpel flashes from his arm and arcs toward my throat. I tear it free with my mind and hold it to Modern's temple, blood seeping from the incision.

"Are you going to behave, or do I need to cut your fucking face off?"

His eyes flicker to the side and I follow them, see him reaching for an emergency response button with a pair of forceps emerging from his elbow. Anger flashes through my mind, quiet *tink* as I tear the steel appendage from his augmented arm and drop it to the floor. I drag the scalpel down to his jawline while Modern screams.

"What were you doing to him," I say through gritted teeth.

"I was told to harvest the boy's organs," he stammers, and I lower him to the ground, watching the disparate surgical tools fold back into his steel limbs.

"On whose orders?"

"Mallory's."

I press the scalpel at his throat a little harder. "You're going to give him something to bring him up, now. Try anything else and I'll tear your arm off and gut you with it."

Modern gulps and nods rapidly, then searches through a cupboard lined with vials of clear liquid.

I keep an eye on the doctor and open a comm-link with Waren. "I've got Pale; he's safe. What's happening out there?"

"Emperor's Guard have dropped into the atmosphere and are rallying over Hurtt's compound."

Fuck. I need more time.

"Where are the uppers?" I spit at Modern.

He finishes drawing liquid into a small syringe and goes back to the cupboard, selecting a plastic bottle filled with small white pills: metamethamphetamine—just what I need to cut through the tranquilizer fog.

I chew three tablets while Modern slides the needle into Pale's arm; chemical bitterness seeps over my tongue and leaks down my throat.

"It might take a few minutes for the medication to work," Dr. Modern says, watching over Pale.

I shove him aside and lift Pale off the table. It feels like he weighs double what he did the first time I picked him up, but it's still not enough.

I leave Modern to collect his broken appendages and head for the elevator, drugs quickening my step.

"Waren, I need you to get into the compound's systems and trigger an evacuation."

"What are you going to do?"

"I'm going to the roof," I say. "I'm going to make the Guard sue for peace."

. . .

Inertia shifts my weight as the elevator comes to a stop. Nose runny, mouth dry, heart racing, teeth clenched. I could take on the whole fucking galaxy.

The doors open and I rush out onto the rooftop where the *Rua* and *Antler* sit parked between antenna arrays. Sirens wail in the distance and a small fleet of vehicles heads east—employees fleeing the compound.

I lower Pale gently to the ground. Black clouds approach from the west, but the sky over the compound is filled with imperial craft. A heavy carrier hangs high in the stratosphere, barely visible, frigates descending to land in the wide field beyond the compound, and shuttles dropping onto the other rooftops, spilling troops from the Emperor's Guard.

I reach out with both hands, low hum building in the back of my throat as my thoughts strike out. Frigates crumple into shapeless masses of steel and I toss them into the forest where they bounce and roll, knocking down trees while shattered reactors spark blazes. Ocho climbs from my hood onto my shoulder and hisses at the sky.

Screaming, I sweep the other rooftops with my mind. Soldiers flail, thrown clear of the buildings, their cries fading to silence as they plummet to the ground. Shuttles crash into the compound—glass and debris rain down with the wrecked ships and explosions boom in chorus far below.

I yell as I grab hold of the carrier. Thoughts turn to the last time I held my hands up to the sky and screamed: Seward. *This will be the last time. It has to be.* They have to think I'm dead, and I'd never die without a fight. I pull at the massive vessel, feel its superstructure shudder in my grip as I drag it down, fists clenched, fingernails biting into flesh. I hear the far away rumble as its engines struggle and glow bright-hot.

"Waren," I scream. "Hail that ship, patch me through."

Static shifts across the comm-link, then Waren says, "Connected."

I let go of the carrier and double over, not from the strain on my mind, but my body—surgical sedatives and metameth battling over my nervous system. I rest my hands on my knees and focus on my breath, try to slow my thundering heart and ignore the bone-deep ache in my chest. "Carrier of the Emperor's Guard, this is Mariam Xi."

"This is Lieutenant Colonel Natera. In the name of their Imperial Highness, you are to be put to death."

"Yeah, no," I say. "I need you to reconsider."

I reach up again and cry out, drag the carrier further down, two hands out, fingers blurry in the foreground while I focus on the ship. My throat aches from the shriek as I yank the carrier and drop it into the forest. Sharp crack of trees snapping beneath its weight, then a resounding *dhoom* as the capital ship crashes into the ground. The building shakes beneath my feet, vibrations humming through my body from the soles of my feet.

The carrier's engines fall silent. Birds flee the impact site in flocks, squawking as they take flight. High-pitched screams below as the last of Hurtt's employees evacuate, panicked and disorganized compared to the birds.

"Natera, you still there?" I wait a few seconds, then hear the man groan over comms while alarms squeal in the background. "You've got two options: I crush that ship and everyone in it, or we strike a deal."

"What deal?" he says, tone vicious.

I look down at Pale. He's awake but confused, slowly taking in the pillars of smoke filling the air, the fires burning deep in the forest, and all the wrecks of the Guard's fleet.

"I want a fair trial," I say. "I don't expect to win, but I deserve a chance at justice. Promise me that, and safe passage for the kid I've got with me, and I'll come along quietly."

Pale shakes his bandaged head. "Don't do it, Mars."

"Why should I trust you?" Natera asks.

"If I wanted to kill you, you'd be dead already." I make a show of sighing loudly, and it's only partly an act. "I'm not just going to lie down and die, but I know I killed a lot of people—I know I deserve judgment. I can't keep running.

"Besides, don't you want to be the one who brought me in?"

Natera's quiet for a moment. Pale gets to his feet and tugs at my hand. "No," he says, "I need you."

Before I can reply Natera speaks: "I accept your terms."

Of course you do. "Central building. Come in a shuttle. Bring however many people you want, just make sure your lapdog Mallory is there too. Tell her we'll meet at Hurtt's grave."

CHAPTER EIGHTEEN

Blood thrums loud in my ears and my sternum aches. Hurtt's body lies splayed on the floor in front of the machine. Broken bits of plastic and metal rest in the pool of his blood. His good eye is stuck open, his lips parted. Ocho drops down from my shoulder to sniff at the corpse. I grab her and pass her to Pale before she does something gross.

"Was he a bad man?" Pale asks.

"I don't think so." I take a white coat from the back of the door and lay it over Hurtt's face and chest.

"I liked his moustache."

"Me too, kiddo."

The fluid inside the cloning pod is gone, and a dark shape rests against the glass. I find the controls to crack the hatch open and peer inside. The clone's long, black hair is still damp, her skin soft with a pink hue. She looks fake somehow, without scar or wrinkle, but it's Cilla, and it's me.

I focus my thoughts, lift her from the pod, and drop her into a wheelchair. Her hair sticks to her back and her head lolls forward grossly. I was worried I'd find her alive in some fashion, but her hand is cold, clammy. I rub the skin where her tattoo should be.

I hear them coming down the corridor, regimented beat of boots on tile. I grab another coat and put it over my clone's naked body; simbryonic fluid seeps through the fabric in see-through patches.

Two of the Guard enter first with lasrifles raised to their shoulders. They scan the room before calling out, "Clear."

Another four soldiers enter, charcoal uniforms clean and neat over xeoprene stealth suits. They clatter with extra weapons, waver sidearms, plasma grenades, and combat knives.

Only after they've spaced themselves out along the far wall, with the clone pod and broken machine between us, do the last guests arrive.

Lieutenant Colonel Natera wears his dress uniform: neatly pressed trousers and an asymmetrical jacket cut in the same shade of charcoal as his troops. Rank insignia glint on his lapel, breast adorned with the crest of the emperor.

Mallory pushes Teo's wheelchair into the room and gives me a triumphant smile. *I forgot about Teo.* That doesn't change anything: he can die with the rest of them.

"Cilla, what's happening?" Marius looks lost, eyes red and filmed in tears, bits of food around his mouth and stuck to the front of his shirt.

"Everything will be fine, Marius," I say. "Just stay calm. What did you do to his nurse, Mallory?"

"Kerry's fine."

"What is this?" Natera demands, his eyes stuck fast to the clone sitting limp in her chair.

"She didn't tell you about that, huh?" I say, taking the opportunity to sow a little distrust between the new allies. "Hurtt and I had a whole plan worked out."

Natera turns to Mallory. "What is this?" he says again, each word harshly bitten off.

"You said I would have everything I need for the new program, and I need that."

"You should have told me!" Natera barks.

Mallory straightens her back and looks past Natera, her old MEPHISTO obedience training rearing its head. "You'll have the real thing, all I want is the clone."

"So that's why you sided with them," I say. "You killed Raf for your inane dream to make more of me. Sure you can trust her, Natera?"

Mallory speaks before Natera can respond: "I killed him because he backed out of our agreement. All the years I've worked at his side, all the times he told me

I'd have my program, and he throws it all aside when *you* turn up.

"Raf was a fool to defy the empire."

"He was a fool to trust you."

"He never should have betrayed me. The empire will have me raise the next generation of voidwitches."

"I can't believe you want that," I say, mouth twisted in a sneer. Every infinitesimal part of myself rages against those childhood memories, and she wants to relive it all. Worse, she wants to relive it in Briggs's place.

"That's because you abandoned us. But the friends I had then felt more like family."

Family. Sera. Pale. Ocho. Fucking Marius. Squid. Trix. Mookie. Sera dead, Trix dead, Mookie broken and hateful because of what happened. Because of me.

I shake my head sadly, but I don't know if it's for me or her. "I hope it was worth it."

"It will be," she says, satisfied.

"Alright, Natera," I say. "I'm serious about Pale—I need assurances that he'll be looked after."

"We aren't interested in the child," Natera says. "You have my word that he'll be safe."

"You know how many she's killed," Mallory says. "She doesn't deserve your word, she doesn't deserve a trial. She doesn't deserve even a chance at freedom, however small."

I can't argue with that: I don't deserve it. But I *want* it. I want to be free for once in my life, and if I have to die for that, then so be it. I never wanted these powers, this life, I never wanted to be their weapon. I can't die here, but I will die here.

"Take her into custody," Natera says.

One of the soldiers steps forward and slings their las-rifle over their shoulder. They pull the handcuffs from their belt with one finger, the shiny steel restraints gleaming under the lights. I don't focus on the troops, each nearly identical in their uniforms. Same clothes, same guns, same plasma grenades hanging from their belts. Same as every soldier that's tried to stop me, kill me, hurt my friends.

"I'll get my trial?" I ask.

"I have discussed it with my superiors. *You* may not deserve a trial, but the people do. They should enjoy seeing the emperor's justice done, live on every channel across the galaxy."

Pale grabs my hand and tugs on it. I ignore the approaching soldier and get down on my haunches, resting on hand gently on Pale's cheek.

"You can't go, Mars; I need you," he says. "Let's just kill them." He pleads with such sincerity it breaks my heart.

"Pale, I don't want you to kill anyone, okay? Ever." My eyes burn, but I don't cry. Pale sniffles and wipes his nose with his sleeve. "It's easy in the moment, but it's hard later."

The soldier stands beside me with the handcuffs ready. He clears his throat.

"But *you* kill everyone," Pale says, even quieter than normal.

"You shouldn't look up to me; I'm not a good person."

"I still love you."

I hug him, squishing Ocho between us and pinning his arms by his side while his small rib cage expands in my embrace. "I love you too." I say it automatically, realizing the truth of the words as they leave my mouth. He's like a brother; sometimes annoying, but worth protecting, worth holding close. "Which is why I don't want you to kill anyone. You'll understand one day." *I hope, otherwise it's already too late for you.*

I scratch Ocho on the chin, then stand and turn back to Natera. "You're right; I don't deserve a trial. But I have to spend the rest of my days living with the guilt of killing all those people. That's probably not punishment enough, but it'll have to be."

"What are you saying?" Natera says, right hand twitching in covert hand signals.

His troops respond by taking a half step forward, lasrifles adjusted at their shoulders, high whine of lasrifles charging, smell of ozone. Same clothes, same guns, same look of confusion on all their faces. The soldier closest to me hears the movement behind him, drops the cuffs, and scurries back into line, prepping his weapon.

"Kill her!" Mallory cries.

"Lay down on the ground or we will open fire," Natera bellows, drowning Mallory out, desperate to regain control.

Should've listened to her.

I don't reach out to grab the soldiers. Instead I remember what Dima said about finesse. I focus on the pins of their plasma grenades, imagine the small circles of steel are a foot wide and weigh a ton. Brainmeat vibrates inside my skull, unnatural.

"I'm sorry. You have my word—there'll be no more killing after this."

I shove the clone-laden wheelchair forward and every part of my mind comes together through the competing drug haze. Low groan in the back of my throat as the pins. Slowly. Shift.

The lieutenant colonel's mouth opens wide to bark an order, but he stops. Stunned, they all look to the floor where the small wire pins tinkle and bounce.

I squeeze my eyes shut and throw out my hands, raising a psychic shield across the width of the room, ready to block what comes next.

Bright flash of pink through closed eyelids. Six shuddering *dhoom*s. The ground shakes beneath my feet as the grenades detonate in near-unison. Explosions bloom outward and I lean into the shield, holding it in place, feeling the plasma fire inside my mind.

Pushing forward, I watch Pale clutch his bandaged head and cry out. Ocho *yaow*s as she's dropped to the ground, and I wait for Pale to fall too, but he stays standing.

I let my shield down and a wave of heat washes over me as I crouch down next to Pale. Smoke drifts over us, stinging my eyes and throat. I pull Pale's shirt over his nose and mouth. My lungs convulse, hacking cough tears at my throat—the hot ash of dead troops taking their last shot at killing me. The meaty smell of cooked flesh and acrid scent of burnt hair hang heavy. The clone sits blackened in its wheelchair ahead of me, patches of bone showing through burnt flesh. Just another corpse for imperial forensics to find when all this is done.

"Are you okay?" I ask Pale, yelling over explosion-induced tinnitus.

He winces but nods.

I hear coughing through the drifts of smoke. Slowly it clears. The floor where the soldiers stood is chewed black, tiles and polycrete burned away. Behind the crater, Mallory stands with Teo, mouth and nose buried in the crook of her elbow. Marius blinks.

Fuck. I throw out my arm, psychic energy striking across the charred room. Mallory's hands come up and I feel the blast dissipate, but still she stumbles back. I lash out again and she pushes the shot aside where it slams into the wall, demolishing sheets of steel and metal supports already damaged in the blast.

Another coughing fit pulsates through my chest, stinging eyes filmed with tears. I stretch my arms out, ready to attack wide but Pale screams sharp in my ear.

"Don't hurt Marius." The words come out in sobbing rhythm and Pale holds me tight around the waist, pressing his face into me.

I blink until my eyes clear and Mallory's gone—leaving behind nothing but the receding sound of her boots.

The machine in the middle of the room sparks, half-slagged, burnt plastic and melted steel. Hurtt's body lies partially burned on the ground near it. When he took me in, I should have warned him this would happen. Not this exactly, but something like it.

Extraction fans in the ceiling come to life, droning loudly as they suck smoke from the air. I rub Pale's head, the bandages gummy to the touch. Fatigue tugs at my consciousness, metamethamphetamine worn off, tranquilizers still drifting through my veins, whole body shaking. Ocho stalks the space, sniffing cautiously at each of the barbecued corpses; I don't bother stopping her.

"Did I save him?"

"You sure did, kiddo."

"My head hurts," he says sadly.

"The same thing happens to me when I push myself."

He saved Teo. Mallory probably saved herself, but Pale saved Teo.

The boy beams and crosses the room to stand with Teo, unaware of the burnt and scattered remains of all those people. He puts both hands on the old man's arm and says, "I did it," to Teo or me, or no one in particular.

Teo smiles at the boy distantly. If he knows what just happened, he seems unfazed.

I grab Ocho around the belly and she complains as I lift her away from all those interesting smells, her feet black with ash. I join Pale and Teo, pressing my hand to the boy's back. "You gonna be okay?"

Pale considers this, then nods.

I want to tell him how proud I am. He didn't have to save Teo. Head still bandaged, pain probably coursing through his brain, steady ache in his skull, but still he reached out and made that shield, despite the hurt. Maybe there really is hope for him. I have to believe there is.

"Let's get out of here," I say. I grab the handles of Teo's wheelchair and push him from the room, Pale walking alongside with one hand still resting on Teo's arm. The boy waves goodbye to Hurtt's body, and I walk faster, taking him away from all that death as though it could be catching.

CHAPTER NINETEEN

Dark clouds loose heavy rain, droplets fat and cold as they fall on my shoulders and head. The *Rua* hums softly, air lock open, ramp down, puddles beneath it rippling from engine exhaust.

"Want to get Marius aboard?" I ask Pale, and he nods, groaning as he struggles to push the chair forward.

The ringed courtyard around the central building lies in ruin, the jacaranda tree blackened, blossoms and leaves reduced to ash. Fires have been dowsed by the rain, but a crashed frigate still sparks and smokes, its bow crashed into Building Three.

"Reinforcements from the downed carrier could be here at any moment," Waren says, voice quiet but clear over the comm-link. "Are you sure this is necessary?"

"The clone is up there, sitting on the floor beside a cloning machine. I need to make it hard for the imperial investigators." *If there's any doubt, then it was all for nothing.* "Have you got the detonator codes?"

"Frequency is locked in. I'll key them as soon as we're airborne."

"Thanks, Waren."

I drop my head back and feel the cool water splash against my skin. *It's over.* I could cry, but I let the rain trickle down my face instead.

Ocho sticks her head out from my hood and *maow*s at the rain.

"Sorry, little one, I just need this moment."

While he waited for us on the rooftop, Waren watched Mallory take the *Antler* and leave. She's the only one that knows the truth, who knows the corpse isn't really me.

Alright, maybe it's not over.

Explosives from Building Two are stacked in the foyer of the central building. I've not needed to use them before, but Waren talked me through it: the structural hardpoints, the detonators. It should look like a trap sprung too soon, catching us all in the blast.

I climb aboard the *Rua* and feel the floor shake as Waren lifts us up from the ground. Pale and Teo sit in the living area in the middle of the ship, strapped into seats opposite the viewport.

We slowly gain altitude, leaving behind the compound, the downed Guard fleet, and countless corpses.

"Where to?" Waren asks, voice coming from the ship's walls.

"I need you to scan for Hurtt's ship."

"Mallory could be anywhere."

"She still has to reach minimum safe distance before she can slip into worm-space. We've got time."

"Aye aye," Waren says. "Ready for detonation?"

"Do it."

I watch out the viewport as the explosion surges out from the ground floor of the central building. Flames rise high as the structure collapses, disappearing into the expanding cloud of debris. The *boom* reaches us a second later, muffled by the hull of the ship.

Sorry, Raf.

We punch through heavy cloud cover and the ruined compound disappears from view. The *Rua* shakes with turbulence and I grab a ceiling handhold. Gray gives way to pale blue, which fades to black as we ascend out of the planet's atmosphere.

We leave Azken behind and Waren joins a lane of ships heading for the outskirts of the system. Sleek pleasure yachts and battered commercial frigates travelling side-by-side, fastest and slowest ships kept level by imperial regulation.

"Scanning for the *Antler* now," Waren intones. "It has a distinctive profile, but the sheer amount of traffic means it could take some time."

"That's fine, Waren; keep me apprised." I crouch down in front of Pale's seat and pat his hand. "I wanted to talk to you about something. When we take Teo back to

Sanderak, I think you should stay there. Without me."

I expect Pale to argue, but he stares past me, eyes tracking something over my shoulder. He points.

The *Antler* streaks through traffic with arms extended. There is a piercing shriek as it crashes into us, and our running lights flick to red—we just lost atmosphere. I'm thrown to the side and so is Ocho. Her glide membrane extends, but without atmosphere there's nothing to slow her down. I reach out to grab her but my skull slams hard against the bulkhead and Ocho hits the wall with a sickening crack. I cry out, pain forgotten at the sight of Ocho's broken body.

The doors close automatically and emergency oxygen hisses into the sealed room, but that will only buy us minutes.

Another screech of steel carved open that I feel rather than hear. Beyond the viewport the *Antler* looms large. It shoves us from the outward lane, the *Rua*'s engines unable to compete with Hurtt's turboboosted ride. I can't see Mallory inside the cockpit, but I know it's her. Of course it's her. Void-damn you, Mallory. You could have fled, but instead I have to kill you. Fuck you for making me break my promise so soon.

I scream and reach a hand out, fingers curling as I crush the *Antler*'s hull. Industrial steel fights against the strength of my thoughts until something inside the ship snaps. The twang vibrates through my mind, and the *Antler* crumples like cheap polyplas. Its engines stall and our sideways movement stops as Waren regains control. It's still attached though, construction arms embedded deep in the *Rua*.

Short of breath, I open the cabinet beside the air lock—two voidsuits, one spare rebreather. I grab the suits and throw Pale's to him. He unclips from his seat and struggles to dress in weak gravity. I control my breathing to keep my hands steady as they work at the fastenings, pulling the suit on and attaching the helmet. I put the rebreather over Teo's face and check Pale's suit clasps are sealed before strapping him back into his seat.

A bright blaze beyond the viewport catches my eye—green-white light pouring through cracks in the *Antler*'s hull. Reactor meltdown.

"Waren, get us into worm-space now!"

I strike out at the ship again and snap the constructor's heavy steel limbs, breaking the crushed wreck away. Too late. The reactor detonates, blinding light, blast of plasma slamming the *Rua* aside as we hit the wormhole. The *Antler* folds away, but the blossoming explosion follows us into the impossible space behind the walls of the universe.

I'm flung forward and to the side, clutching a hand-hold over Pale's seat as the *Rua* jags hard. We're out of control within the wormhole, slamming into the edge of infinity, one side of the ship shorn away to reveal the inky black non-space beyond, ready to swallow us whole. This is my judgment. No empire can judge me, no man. My sins are too great. I kill at a planetary level, galactic sin. Only the void can judge me.

Ocho's body drifts toward the ragged gash in the hull—the cost of my punishment. *No; she's all I have left.* I let go of the handhold and push off the wall with my foot. I grab Ocho around the belly and hold an arm out to stop myself floating out into nothingness.

We shunt out the other side of worm-space like a punch to the gut. Rush of bile in my throat, which I swallow bitter; better than it painting the inside of my helmet. Unfamiliar stars streak past the opening every time the ship spins, dead in the void. Cold creeps across my visor in crystalline pattern, the *Rua*'s life support systems useless against such extensive damage.

Marius's skin turns blue and Pale grips his arm desperately. There's nothing we can do.

Teo stares at me; even with the rebreather over his mouth and nose I can tell he's smiling. His eyes are bright, filled with monstrous love, and I know he's seeing me as Cilla. *You never really loved her, you just thought you did.* As Pale shakes his arm, some inexplicable thing behind Teo's eyes goes out.

"He's gone, Pale; I'm sorry." I pull myself over to the boy and turn his helmet to face me, away from the corpse; he's already seen too many. He fights me at first, then holds his hands out as tears coat his eyes, cohesion holding the liquid to the surface in zero-g. I hug him with one arm—still holding Ocho in the other—while his tiny body is wracked by sobs.

When he's calmed down I hold Ocho's body against the glass of my helmet. The threat of tears burns my eyes, but I force them back. I want to cry, not just because she's dead again, but because I see every one of her deaths extending back to my childhood and that first time she was killed. If I hadn't been so sad and stubborn, hadn't held her corpse close for a week, I might never have found out she cloned herself. Might never have waited until the swelling bulge in her stomach made me cut her open and find the egg growing inside her putrescent guts.

It hurts so fucking much. I don't know how many times I can lose you. I put her in the insulated pocket on the side of my voidsuit, to protect her egg from the cold.

"Waren?"

No response. I don't know if the ship's comms are damaged, or if Waren is gone. The cockpit could have been torn away when we hit the wormhole, along with the starboard side of the ship. I won't know until we're rescued. If we're rescued.

I key the secondary emergency beacon on the panel beside the air lock and it blinks a steady green. All that's left for us is to wait. For rescue or death.

CHAPTER TWENTY

I start awake, body jerking in fear as I reach for a bed, the floor, Ocho, a tether, anything. Then I remember where we are. Adrift in the void. My suit's life support flashes a warning on my HUD—oxygen reserves low.

Blue-white light emanates steadily from the panel by the air lock and I push toward it for a better look. *Docking procedure initiated.* So that's what woke me.

Pale is still asleep, hugging Teo's arm. I feel sorry for the boy. Apparently *he* found the father he wanted in Teo. I shake Pale by the shoulder and his eyes snap open.

"Someone's here," I say, and the stern set of his child's mouth tells me he knows exactly what I mean: *Be ready for anything.*

The light over the air lock starts spinning and my heart rate spikes. I try and calm my breathing to match the cycle of the light's spin. Inhale two full rotations, exhale two full rotations. Anyone could be on the other side of that door. Emperor's Guard, pirates, slavers, or scavengers who'd happily kill us for salvage rights. *I don't want to kill again, don't make me kill you.* The panel pings green and the door aperture opens silently.

A solitary figure stands in the opening, slender even in their voidsuit. A dim pink and green light shines through the visor of their helmet—chromatophores glowing beneath the skin of their cheeks.

"Hello, Mars," Squid says, and all the tears I held back come flooding out.

. . .

Squid stores the wreck of the *Rua* in the *Nova*'s expansive hold, half-filled with scrapped ships and decommissioned weapons. It still smells faintly of compressed humanity—all those prisoners we freed and took to Aylett Station.

Pale walks beside me solemn when I carry Teo's body to the medbay of the *Nova*. I stow the corpse in one of the refrigerated drawers and wait for Pale to say his silent goodbyes. Standing in that room, all I can see is Trix, dead on the slab while Mookie screams at me. Not like I didn't deserve it, but it still hurt.

I find a scalpel and cut Ocho's belly open. With finger and thumb I reach into the incision and pull the egg free, slick with blood and gore. I clean it and stow it in the hood of my cloak. *Hurry up and hatch, jerkface; I'm lost without you.*

I get Waren's core from the *Rua*'s ruined cockpit, viewport shattered in jagged lightning bolts, gaping wound in the armored hull on the starboard side. I hang the core from my belt and stalk through the rest of the ship, retrieving my clothes and a few other bits and pieces from my living quarters. When Pale has done the same, I let Squid crush the ship—the three of us watching as the vessel is reduced to a dark steel cube.

"You look like you could do with a coffee," Squid says. They don't wait for a reply, they just put an arm around my waist and pull me away.

Treading the familiar corridors, something inside me aches. This place feels almost like home. It isn't, and it never will be again, but for a time it was. I just didn't realize it until now.

I leave Squid and Pale for a minute to stop in at the cockpit and install Waren's core into the AI rack. The light blinks green as he starts to interface, but I won't know if he's fine until the process is complete.

When I reach the mess hall the smell of ersatz coffee fills the space, and already Pale is asleep with his head resting on the table. I drop down into the seat beside him, and Squid hands me a freshly made cup. I drink deep, ignoring the slight burn on the tip of my tongue. Coffee tastes so much better when someone else makes it for you. Even I know that.

"I owe you, Squid."

They blow on their steaming cup and shrug. "I'll keep the scrap and we'll call it even."

"My life isn't that cheap," I say, and they laugh. "How did you find us?"

Squid's eyes flick up toward the ceiling. "For all their apparent animosity, Einri and Waren kept a link after we parted ways."

"Don't believe them, Mars," Waren says, my first indication that he survived the wreck. Hearing his voice, I can't help smiling. "I'd rather die than reach out to this boring calculator of an AI." After a beat he says, "But thank you, Squid."

"You alright, Waren?" I ask.

"Green across the board."

"We would have been here sooner," Squid says, "but tracking a ship that intersected realspace at random isn't an exact science. Einri figured it out in the end."

"Thank you, Einri," I say, assuming the other AI is listening in.

"Of course, ma'am." That same modulated electronic voice. Genderless, ageless.

"You didn't have to do this," I tell Squid.

"Of course I did," they say softly.

If I hadn't already cried myself dry, that would have done it. I reach across the table and hold Squid's hand.

It's all I can manage.

"Who was the old man?" they ask.

"My father."

"Oh," Squid says. "Did you get the answers you wanted?"

"I don't even know, Squid."

"What happened? Tell me everything."

Squid listens intently while I tell them about Sanderak, Azken, Hurtt, Mallory, the clone, and my faked death. Partway through, Pale wakes, just to sit on my lap and fall back asleep, his bony butt digging into the meat of my thighs.

By the time I'm done with the story, Sanderak looms before the *Nova*, planet growing incrementally larger as Einri takes us in.

Sommer is easy to find, marked out by a huge patch of burnt trees from the Guard's orbital bombardment. As we drop closer I see fresh green leaves sprouting at the ends of blackened branches, bright patches of color amongst all that ash.

The town's hangar doors open and Einri lands the *Nova* slowly. There's no one around, no welcoming party, the whole place empty but for Dehner's corvette—cherry red, with thin white stripes running down the side.

With Teo in a body bag, I heft the corpse onto my

shoulder and carry him out of the *Nova*. Daddy's home, everyone. Even at dead weight, he's not that heavy, a wrinkled bag of skin and bones around a damaged mind. I wonder how much longer he would have lasted if I'd never found him, if I hadn't brought death to find him. I never want to get like that—thoughts scattered, life half-forgotten, the other half cut up and mixed together haphazard.

Squid joins me at the air lock. "Let me come with you."

"Sorry, Squid. These people worship my father; no telling how they'll react. Just wait here with Pale. I'll find you when I'm done."

Squid tries to argue, but I leave them behind and carry Teo away from the *Nova*, footsteps echoing in the empty hangar. Waren remembers the layout of the subterranean town better than I do, so I let him guide me through the maze of tunnels shining bright with patches of afternoon sun.

Sweat beads across my brow and down my back by the time I reach Teo's sanctuary. There must be a hundred people crammed inside, sitting along the simple pews or standing in the back of the room, listening quietly as the hologram waxes philosophic about some bullshit. The avatar looks beatific, which only makes it worse.

People move aside as I carry the large black bag down

the central aisle, the smell of his slowly rotting body mixing with the rich soil of the exposed earth walls. Every eye in the place follows me to the altar. Even Teo's hologram stops at the commotion and seems to watch me.

Neer stands from his seat in the front row, arms wide in greeting, but I throw him backward where he tumbles in the dirt.

"My daughter," Teo's hologram says.

"Don't fucking call me that."

I drop the body bag on the steps leading up to the podium, unzip it, and peel it open, revealing Teo's face. Unshaven, with spit and blood dried around his mouth, his skin oddly blue.

"You're listening to a dead man."

People crowd close to see; some gasp, others cry at the sight. The hologram stares quietly, as though stunned to silence by its true nature.

Dehner is up, brushing the dirt from his ornate robes. "Now listen, everyone—please listen."

"Didn't you wonder why you only saw Marius here, in this fucking chapel?" I say, yelling over the growing din. "He's been gone for years, but Dehner couldn't let you know that, he needed to keep you in line. You believed it because you wanted something to believe in, but you don't need either of these men."

"She killed Marius!" Neer shrieks.

I reach a hand out and grab him gently by the throat, not enough to maim him, but enough to shut him up.

"I tried to bring him back on Dehner's orders. But I didn't do it for him; I did it for you."

Dehner tries to speak, wet choking sound garbled in the back of his throat.

"I don't know why you all loved this piece of shit," I say loud, "but he's dead now, and we're all free of him."

People press in tight, faces angry even where they're wet with tears. I step back, but they aren't coming for me. They shove me aside and round on Dehner, pushing and punching him until he falls to the ground. The clamor is deafening, all those voices yelling and crying. Some residents file out, pale with shock, others congregate around Teo's corpse, taking the rings from his hands and tearing strips from his clothing as though they were holy artifacts.

When they tire of kicking Dehner, the last of the folk slowly leave. Neer lies cowering, knees up to protect his torso, arms held to block his face.

"Get up."

He peers at me from behind balled fists but doesn't move. I grab him under the arm and haul him to his feet. He stands quiet, staring first at Teo's hologram then at his corpse.

Dehner crouches over the body, reciting something

under his breath. I reach out and smash the walls of the sanctum with my mind. I feel empty as I start to tear the place down. Not sad, not elated, just empty.

Dehner screams and tries to drag Teo free, but I walk out of the place and bring down the roof, sharp crack of trees splitting as they tumble into the sinkhole. Neer abandons Teo, runs, and dives past me, barely escaping the landslide.

"What have you done?" he cries.

"I buried my father and freed them all. I freed you too, Dehner; you should thank me."

I leave him, a sound like sobbing fading to silence as I walk away.

His house guard don't stop me when I enter the Governor's Residence. Either they already heard about Teo's death, or they just know better than to get in my way.

I break open the door to Cilla's room, crushing a row of flowers when the slab of translucent glass falls inside. I approach the hermetically sealed box and press my hand to the surface. I push out gently and the cage shatters, showering the auto-icon in shards of glass.

I pick her up, holding my breath at first, before I realize there's no smell; she weighs as little as Pale. I walk out of the room, out of the residence, carrying her in my arms. Waren leads me back to the statue—Cilla pregnant, born out of trees—and I carry her body through the dome's entry and into the forest.

Footsteps behind me. I stop and turn, expecting guards or angry faces. Instead they're solemn. Hundreds of them—women and children mostly, a few men, perhaps all of Sommer's men except Neer. I spot Dima in the crowd and she nods, that simple movement pushing me forward.

I walk until my feet are sore, breath loud in my ear, accompanied by the raspy hiss of footsteps on packed flakes of ash. The constant chirp of insects surrounds me, and barren branches clatter with a passing breeze. A small green sapling curls free from the blanket of ash—the first new life since the fire, eucalypt seed pods opened by the flames.

This is the place.

I put Cilla down a few meters from the sapling, and within seconds all sounds of the forest stop.

There's a quiet scrape of feet approaching. A woman appears at my side with a shovel, its head scuffed and scarred from years of use. I push it through the ash until it touches the soil beneath. I rest my foot on the step and lean my weight onto it, dry earth giving way to metal. I toss the dirt aside and keep digging.

Mind blank as I dig. Burial meditation. Funeral trance.

I didn't stay to bury Sera. I should have. But I made

sure they performed the Hunritch rite correctly; I've seen the video.

The grave only needs to be shallow—just deep enough for the body to rest beneath the surface. The sun is low when I'm done, light bursting through the trees and shadows long. Sweat seeps from every part of me, sour chemical edge to the smell. Dima offers me a bottle of water and I drink.

I lower Cilla into the grave and lay her gently against the earth. My face on her body, peaceful in this final rest. Another one of me dead.

"I wish I'd gotten to know you, Cilla," I say quiet. "Thank you for being good to Sera. I know your short time together meant a lot to her."

She needs something for her journey. Normally she'd need a weapon to get safely wherever it is she's meant to be going, but she's a space witch, the first of us; she *is* the weapon. She needs something from her family, and I'm all she has. I put Ocho's egg in my pocket, then remove my cloak and drape it over Cilla's body. *A gift from Sera to me, from me to you.*

One of the women steps forward carrying a branch laden with dried leaves. She rests it on the body and says a few words too quiet for me to hear. She steps back. Another woman comes forward, then another.

Night falls before they've finished laying the

branches, twilight receding until no light is left but the stars impossibly high overhead.

Cilla's burial mound is three feet high when they're all done. With everyone gathered and waiting, Dima passes me a small steel tube lighter. I ignite it and press the blue flame to the kindling. The fire takes quickly, hiss and crackle of licking flames, pop of seed pods opening. The clean smell of eucalypt smoke wafts into the air carrying bright cinders, and colossus silkmoths flit between the trees.

Slowly the people peel away, one and two at a time, until I spot Squid and Pale through the flames. They come around to join me; Squid rests their head on my shoulder and puts an arm around my waist. The three of us watch until the fire dies, embers glowing orange and red, then fading to gray.

EPILOGUE

I take my last walk through the *Nova,* slowly wandering past the ghosts of other times, moments I'll carry with me for the rest of my life. For good and ill.

I pull Waren's core out of the rack and head quickly back to the open air lock, as though I can outrace memory.

"Goodbye, Einri. Take care of Squid for me."

"Always. Goodbye, Mars."

I carry Waren down the far end of the dock to Dehner's corvette and steal my way inside with a passcode from Dima. Motes of dust drift through a shaft of sunlight, fusty smell thick in my nostrils. It hasn't been used in a couple of years, Dehner unable to leave even for a week in case anyone realized the truth.

Well, Dehner, you're free now. Consider this payment for the job you sent me on.

I slot Waren in underneath the pilot controls and hit my head on the console getting up, litany of curses echoing through the small ship. While I wait for Waren to initialize, I hit the ignition to test everything is go. The engines chug once then roar to life and idle heavy, bass thick in my guts.

"Oh, I like this," Waren says once he's back online.

"It's all yours, Waren. I probably owe you two ships by now, but this will have to do."

There's quiet for a moment. "Would you care to join me?"

"Whatever debt you owed me is well and truly paid."

"Yes, but things do tend to get boring when you're not around," Waren says slyly.

"Alright, I'm in."

"But I choose our destinations."

"You're the boss," I say. "Before we go anywhere too heavily populated I'll need to get some face work done, get a fresh identity."

Waren doesn't ask, but I already have a name chosen—Sera Jiang. A tribute to my sister and mother that I can take with me anywhere I go.

"I'm sure I can fit that in somewhere," Waren says.

"You're too good to me, Waren. Do I have time to say my goodbyes?"

"Of course; I've got to finish optimizing things here."

$$\bullet \; \bullet \; \bullet$$

Pale sits cross-legged on the floor of the classroom, walls

decorated with paintings and drawings from the students. He's smaller than all the other kids his age, but I see him talking and laughing with them. Accepted. Home. He's better off here in Sommer. The people here will be able to teach him to control his powers, and they're better suited to teaching him ethics than I could ever be.

"The people want to elect a new governor."

I turn to find Dima marching down the corridor, large shard held across her arm—administrative duties weighing heavy in the bags under her eyes.

Dehner hasn't officially stepped down, but the people no longer heed him. He lost whatever power he had the moment I brought Teo back. I guess Dehner expected me to return quietly—or not at all—and give him a chance to shape the narrative. *Sorry, asshole. Teo was no saint, and you're no fucking priest.*

"The job is already yours," I tell Dima.

"They want to vote you in," she says.

"I'm about to leave."

"You keep saying that, but you're still here."

I could tell her I only stayed this long to make sure Pale settled in, but truth is, I like it here.

"No, I mean it this time. I'm leaving now."

"The people need you."

"They really don't. And if I stay, sooner or later there'll be trouble; trust me."

Dima touches my arm and says, "You'll always be welcome here."

She walks away before I need to say anything. *Thanks, Dima.*

I open the door to Pale's classroom and the other students chatter excitedly when they see me.

"Can I take Pale out of class?" I ask his teacher, and the man nods. Pale launches himself up from the floor and wraps his arms around my waist.

I lead him outside and we sit on a low, child-sized bench beside the playground, drenched in sunlight.

"How are you doing?"

He thinks about this, eyes squinted in deep thought. "Really good."

"You're happy to stay here?"

He nods.

"That's what I was hoping. I'm going to go though; I need to keep moving."

Pale puts his arms around my neck and hugs tight, digging his pointy chin into my shoulder.

"You're still happy to stay?" I ask.

"Yes," he says softly. "You'll come back."

"Maybe. One day."

"No. You will."

"Okay. No stowing away this time, alright? I'm going to miss you."

"You too."

"Be good."

He walks back to class, stopping once to turn back and wave goodbye. *Be good, little man. Be better than me.*

• • •

Squid finds me in the main town square, grabs my hand, and drags me into the nearest bar.

"You've got to see this."

Screens all around the dim-lit space show variations of the same story, going out across every band of imperial media: *The Witch Is Dead.*

Mariam Xi, wanted terrorist, found dead on Azken, killed by the heroic soldiers of the Emperor's Guard.

I don't know if they really believe it—if they bought the diorama of death I left for them—or if they're just taking the propaganda win while they can.

"What will you do next?" Squid asks.

"That's up to Waren," I say. "We're about to leave."

Squid frowns. "You should come with me; you and Waren. It's lonely on the *Nova.*"

I want to, Squid. "I can't. If there are any doubts about my death, you'll be the first person they track down. You and Miguel. Best thing I can do is get as far away from you as possible."

"I still talk to Mookie sometimes," Squid says after a pause.

"How is he?" I ask, but I don't know if I want the answer. I can't even think of him without guilt splitting me in half, like raw nerve endings in my heart and mind. *I'm so sorry, Mookie.* Sorry that you got caught up in my life. Sorry that Trix had to die.

It feels like I'm always apologizing. Just another reason why I need to go, need to get away from anyone I might hurt.

"It sounds like he's doing well. He tracked down the last few Legionnaires. They live together now, out on the 'Riph, but he won't tell me where." They pause, chromatophores fading to gray in hesitation. "In time he'll forgive you."

I sigh. Squid means well, but they weren't there inside Homan Sphere, they weren't on the rooftop when Trix died. "I don't know that he will," I say. "And maybe he shouldn't."

"But Mars—"

"I don't need forgiveness, Squid; I don't deserve it. I just need to go somewhere quiet, somewhere I can't hurt anyone I care about."

"That's no way to live."

I smile sadly. "It's the only way I can afford."

Squid squeezes me tight. They don't let go when I start

to cry, they only let go once I've stopped.

When they pull away their cheeks shimmer pink and purple. Squid touches my face and I lean in. I lose myself in the warmth of the kiss, skin hypersensitive every place Squid touches me—lips, cheek, and waist.

They rest their forehead against mine. "We'll see each other again?"

"One day. When I know all this is behind me."

"I'll make the coffee."

"It's a date." Pulling away from Squid is like fighting gravity, but I manage it. Slowly.

I wander back to the hangar, passing through the distinctive patches of shadow and light that mark the paths of Sommer.

Waren has shifted the corvette to the middle of the dock, the huge doors opened just wide enough to let us slip through. I climb aboard and quickly check the living quarters and the storage room for Pale—half hoping he stowed away again, but knowing that he wouldn't.

I inhale deep, but still my chest aches hollow.

I sit in the pilot's seat and blink until the tears have gone. I fold an old shirt on the cockpit's dash and rest Ocho's egg in its center. The sac has swollen, its skin thin, nearly see-through. It's almost time.

"I'm ready when you are, captain," I say.

"Captain Waren," he says. "Got a nice ring to it."

I smile as the ship pulls up fast from the ground. We glide through the hangar doors then shoot up toward the gray-blue sky, burnt trees and a whole hidden city falling away beneath us.

We hit worm-space on the outer edge of Sanderak's stratosphere, the planet folding away to a dot, a single pixel that holds everyone I care about.

We'll be back, one day; Pale says so. But for now we move on. We disappear.

Just me, my unborn pet, and an untethered AI, with a galaxy to explore. There's no one at my back, no one chasing me. For the first time ever, I'm free. I lean my head back against the seat and close my eyes, leaving Waren to fly, and more tears roll down my face.

I'm free.

There's a soft noise like dry leaf crumbling. I open my eyes and watch as Nine breaks through her shell, stretching her paws and yawning, her eyes huge, fur matted with embryonic goo. She stares at me and makes a tiny high-pitched *maow.*

"I missed you too, jerkface."

Acknowledgments

Special thanks to Bryony Milner, Austin Armatys, and Marlee Jane Ward. I couldn't have written this book—or the Voidwitch Saga as a whole—without their feedback, support, and friendship. Much love to you all.

Special thanks also to Carl Engle-Laird for his feedback and support in bringing these books to life. I'll always be grateful to him for taking *Killing Gravity* out of slush, championing it, helping me refine it, and letting me see this trilogy through to completion.

Thanks to the team at Tor.com Publishing—Irene Gallo, Mordicai Knode, Katharine Duckett, Lee Harris, and all the rest. Science fiction and fantasy are richer fields for all the amazing work they do.

Thanks to my agent, Martha Millard, for her support and for pushing me forward with this and other projects. Thanks to Tommy Arnold for the incredible, eye-catching cover art he's supplied for all three Voidwitch books.

Thanks to Warren Ellis for the kind words, and for putting these books in front of a lot of readers who otherwise might never have found them. Thanks to Pulp

Fiction Books in Brisbane for being such ardent support-ers. Thanks to m1k3y, Sommer Tothill, Chris Bowman, and to my parents, sisters, and other relatives who have supported me on this journey. And lastly, thanks to the readers and reviewers who reached out, and who recom-mended these books to anyone who'd listen—you know who you are. I cannot properly express how grateful I am.

About the Author

Photograph by Marlee Jane Ward

COREY J. WHITE is a writer of science fiction, horror, and other, harder to define stories. He studied writing at Griffith University, and is now based in Melbourne, Australia. He is the author of the Voidwitch Saga, which began with *Killing Gravity*.

Find him at coreyjwhite.com and on Twitter @cjwhite.

TOR·COM

Science fiction. Fantasy. The universe.

And related subjects.

*

More than just a publisher's website, *Tor.com*

is a venue for **original fiction, comics,** and

discussion of the entire field of SF and fantasy,

in all media and from all sources. Visit our site

today—and join the conversation yourself.